# INFATUATION

A NOVEL OF QUESTIONABLE TASTE

## JONATHAN HARRIES

PUBLISHED BY FASTPENCIL PUBLISHING

D1361800

Infatuation

First

Print edition ISBN: 9781499904512

Copyright © Jonathan Harries 2018

http://www.fastpencil.com

Printed in the United States of America

# TABLE OF CONTENTS

# PROLOGUE

*The saloon of the Occidental Hotel in Buffalo, Wyoming, present day.*

I doubt walking in on Butch Cassidy playing poker with Calamity Jane and Teddy Roosevelt would have surprised me more than seeing my old friend, Charley Brooks, perched on a barstool, drinking coffee and reading the *Buffalo Bulletin*. Yet there he was, his big shoulders hunched over, his thick black hair disheveled, swishing his coffee around in his mouth, just the way I remembered him from twenty years before.

I stopped, took a deep breath, and walked over to the man I'd thought of as my closest friend since elementary school. That was until he vanished one day. As mysteriously as mist before the sun.

"Charley...?"

He looked up slowly, almost as if he didn't recognize his own name, peered at me through hooded eyes, shook his head in disbelief, and stood up.

"Good God, Barney? What the hell are you doing here?"

"I was going to ask you the same question, Charley. What happened to you? Where have you been for the last twenty years?"

He opened his arms and, grabbing me in a massive bear hug, started to laugh.

"Oh, Barney, how good it is to see you, old man. Come sit down and tell me all about yourself, and then if you've got the time, I'll tell you the strangest story you've ever heard."

I remembered Charley's stories from his days as a war correspondent, and while they'd always seemed slightly exaggerated, they were usually enormously entertaining. "Time I have, Charley. My golf game's been cancelled because of the storm last night, so I'm on my own. Why don't we grab those chairs over there by the wall and talk? I've missed the hell out of you and I am, I'll admit, more than a little peeved that you never contacted me."

"I've missed you too, Barney, and I am so very sorry that I did disappear like that without letting you know what happened. But I promise when I tell you my story, you'll understand. You may not believe it, I warn you, but you will understand. First, though, I want to hear about you. How are Debbie and your girls? They must be grown up by now."

"Debbie left me ten years ago for a son-of-a-bitch she met in the park while walking the dogs. Took half the money. I guess she was entitled to it, but still I hope they both rot in hell. The girls, on the other hand, are both happily married to nice guys. No grandkids yet. And that's about it. Rather boring, I'm afraid."

He laughed. "Don't knock boring, my friend. Boring doesn't get you killed." He paused as if he were remembering something. Then he smiled and squeezed my shoulder. "Well, sorry about Debbie, although I can probably say this now: I never liked her. She was very mean to you. Always putting you down. Not my business, but I can't think why you stuck with her so long. Anyway, I'm so glad your girls are good, and no doubt you'll be a grandad soon enough. So how about you? Are you still working?"

"Good God, no. I sold the business last year. Made enough to live comfortably. So long as I die by the time I turn eighty-seven, according to my accountant. I'm sixty-one, Charley, and I can definitely feel things beginning to go."

He laughed at that, and I noticed there were no lines around his mouth or eyes. I almost asked him how old he was now, which would have been an odd thing to have asked, because Charley and I were the same age. Yet when I glanced in the mirror behind the bar, I saw two very different men reflected back at me. One was old, fat, and bald, and the other ... well, let's just say there was something very distinct about the other. I shivered despite the warmth of the room. Then I looked into Charley's eyes, wondering what exactly it was that had happened to him since I'd last seen him. Twenty years before. The day he left for Chicago.

# CHAPTER 1

The library in the Palazzo Di Arcieri, Rome, 1998.
*In which unrequited lust gives way to wretched confusion.*

Eduardo Sabatini was aroused.

It was not an unfamiliar state for the scion of one of Italy's most nefarious crime families when in the company of a member of the opposite sex. What was unusual for the slightly dim-witted twenty-four-year-old was that his concupiscence was being severely tempered by an overpowering sense of confusion. The object of both his lust and befuddlement was a large woman with blazing red hair who had, in defiance of his advances, plonked herself down in one of the dark green leather armchairs at the opposite end of the library. She was a belly dancer named Fanny Packer. Most people assumed it was her stage name, and were surprised to learn that it was the one she'd been given twenty-nine years before, when she'd slipped out of her mom's well-worn vagina in the upstairs room of an old brothel near Big Lake, Texas. Eduardo covered his face with his hands and gave a frustrated sigh. What was wrong with her? Couldn't she see what she was giving up by refusing to sleep with him?

He stood up and walked to the ornate mirror fixed to the wall just below a portrait of his great-great grandfather, the first Marchese di Custoza. The Sabatini family, one of the oldest in Rome, occupied half a page in the newer Almanach de Gotha, despite having lacked a noble title for hundreds of years before Mauro Gianlucca Sabatini was made a marchese by King Vittorio Emanuele II following the Battle of Custoza in 1866, during the third Italian War of Independence. The heroic deed for which he was elevated to the ranks of other august Italian heroes had been to remain on the battlefield approximately five minutes longer than his hastily retreating compatriots. Whether it had been an act of bravery or inebriation was never determined.

Eduardo stared up at the painting and then down at his own reflection. There was no question in his mind that he possessed everything that had made generations of Sabatini men famous philanderers and lotharios. He was tall and quite well built, with thick wavy black hair, sharp cheekbones, and soft brown eyes. He might have been considered handsome but for his nose, which, once a perfect specimen of his ancient family's most distinguished feature, now lay slightly askew above a pencil mustache. When anyone asked, he would say it was mangled in a rather unpleasant encounter with Cali Cartel enforcers during his gap year with the Chicago mafia. In reality, he was disfigured during a fall down the stairs of a villa near Lucca, after having consumed two bottles of 1972 Sassacaia with a middle-aged though still insatiable contessa wearing nothing but thigh-high riding boots with sharp silver spurs. Her husband had returned unexpectedly, and was perhaps justifiably more upset about the wine, which was aging rather better than his wife.

Eduardo had always been more a runner than a fighter. This made him an even greater disappointment to his uncle—an unreasonable man to be sure—who thought of Eduardo as a nincompoop, and thus an embarrassment to the great name of Sabatini.

Fanny lowered her head so that her long red curls covered her face as the object of her antipathy walked up behind her and placed his hand on her shoulder. He stroked her arm in an almost loving gesture, and then, taking the ample flesh between his thumb and forefinger, squeezed it gently.

"Ow, you beast!" she whispered under her breath.

"Ow? Ow? Is that a response to a gesture of love? And I did not touch your breast." His accent was a strange combination of hard Irish, learned at the knee and over the knee of his Irish-Catholic governess—an ex-nun expelled from the Vatican for lewd behavior with a Swiss Guard—and nasally Midwestern inflection, thanks to that year abroad attempting to learn the family trade under John 'No Nose' DiFronzo, a cousin of his late mother.

"Well I'm not sure what you want me to say. Look at my arm, it's all red?"

"It's not in the least bit red, but allow me to kiss it better." Eduardo lowered his face and tried to kiss the ample flesh, but she twisted away, causing him to overbalance.

"Fanny," he said as he attempted to recover some dignity, "why won't you make love to me? My heart is sore ... my body aches for you. Here, feel." He tried to put her hand on his crotch, but she pulled away.

"That's very rude, Mr. Sabatini. If you try that again, I'll slap your face."

"Yes, please," Eduardo replied, closing his eyes. "I should like that very much."

"For me to slap your face?"

"Yes, I would, and anything else you'd like to do will be very welcome."

"Well, not to me. You seem like a very sick man, Mr. Sabatini. Perhaps you should see a psychiatrist."

Eduardo took a step back and ground his teeth in frustration. "How can demonstrating my great desire for you be rude or sick?"

"I think you have the wrong idea about belly dancers, you know. I'm a professional. The agreement you signed with my agent was very specific about that."

"Oh, really? You think? The agreement I signed specifies that you would do anything I wanted."

"I believe that referred to my dance routines. And for your information, in case you were unaware, belly dancing, certainly the kind I do, is not meant to be in the least bit sexual. It's about storytelling." She blushed in embarrassment.

"Well, clearly I was unaware of that. But I will ask you to perhaps broaden your storytelling."

"What do you mean, Mr. Sabatini?"

"Well, you know the story of the 1001 Arabian nights? A very erotic story to be sure. Maybe you could tell that story...."

"No, absolutely not. I certainly know the story, and it's totally inappropriate. I'm really sorry, but my mind is made up. I will dance for you but nothing else."

Eduardo took one more look at her and decided that he would never understand American women. Fanny was magnificent. Her hair and body shape were a perfect match for the illuminated illustrations in the ancient text. The only element missing was her failure to comprehend the situation and cooperate. The resulting confusion was causing Eduardo all manner of distress. He took a deep breath to calm himself.

"Fanny," he said softly, "let me try this again. I need to have sex with you very badly. It is very important for my family. I can make you very happy, I promise. Not only am I an excellent lover, but I will buy you many beautiful things. I bet you didn't know that Gucci made dresses in your size. Come, be reasonable. You are very desirable."

Fanny looked into his eyes. She hadn't noticed quite how deep and sad they were. "No, absolutely not. I told you I refuse to have sex, and there's nothing you can say or offer me to change my mind. And I don't care if Gucci makes dresses my size. They

don't sell Gucci at Walmart, and that's where I prefer
to shop."

Eduardo shook his head. This woman was impossible. Yet she was also perfect. His uncle, had he been
present, would have urged him to force himself on
Fanny, then called him a weakling and ninny for his
failure to do so. But Eduardo's mother, an extremely
strong woman, had taught him—before her untimely
death—that violence towards women was abhorrent.
Eduardo respected his mother's memory too much
to go against that. And in any case his sexual predilection, possibly fueled by his governess's domi-
neering nature, lay in another direction entirely. He
contemplated his options for a few seconds before
finally deciding he was wasting his time. There must
be thousands of large redheads out there who fit
the description in the book. He'd just have to get his
agent to extend the search. His uncle would understand.

"Okay, if you can't and won't have sex with me and
you fail to see how happy I could make you, then I'm
afraid I must ask you to leave my library, and then my
palazzo, and then my country."

"Oh, I'm going, don't you worry." Fanny stood up
with every intention of leaving as quickly as possible.

"No, stay right here while I go to make arrangements for your return home. And by the way I hope
you are not expecting to be paid for this past month,
because you will be disappointed." He knew he sounded petulant, but he also knew wasting the family's
money was the one thing his uncle wouldn't understand.

"Oh, please," said Fanny, her sobs turning to full-blown tears. "That's not fair, I really need the money. I have to get back to my mother's place in Wyoming. You ... you can't do this."

"Yes, I can, trust me." He took one last look at her and left the library feeling like a total failure and a jerk. He hated to see her hurt, but he had no choice.


"Why?" she asked herself. "Why, why, why does this always happen to me? Just when I think I'm going to be successful at something, I ruin it all." She took a deep breath and thought what her grandma would have said to her. She could see the old woman sitting on the porch of the large whorehouse near Big Lake, drinking bourbon straight from the bottle, scolding her for not standing up to the boy in kindergarten who'd called her 'Fatty Boomsticks.' "You should have smashed that kid in his face with a fire extinguisher and told him to watch his mouth if he ever found his teeth again. You have to stand up for yourself, girl. You're smart, but you don't have much else going for you, unfortunately, so take what you can when you can."

Grandma was right. She needed to stand up for herself and take what was rightfully hers. If Mr. Sabatini wouldn't pay her then she'd darn well take something belonging to him. She walked quickly to the desk and tried to open the drawers, but they were locked. A glance around the room revealed shelves of books, large hideous paintings of Sabatini ancestors and a few sculptures that looked old and possibly worth money but were far too big to lift. She was sure the books were expensive, but she had no idea who'd buy Italian or Latin texts in Wyoming. The desk, on the other hand, had some silver-framed photographs of Eduardo posing with people she didn't know, but she'd have to take all of the frames to make up for what she was owed, and her bag, though big, wasn't big enough.

Then her eyes fell on a small gold paperweight on the desk that looked like a bloated penguin or bat, with eyes that could have been rubies. She tried to pick it up, but it was stuck to the leather inlay. Wiggling it back and forth failed to dislodge it. When she tried to move it side to side, there was a click and a small door on the side of the desk popped open. It was just wide enough for her to reach in and feel around with her hand, and yes, there was something in there that was both thick and soft. Thinking it could be a wallet, she pulled it out and … sighed. Yet another book. It certainly looked older than the others, but it was still a book and her disappointment was palpable. But as she was about to return it to the secret compartment, she heard someone at the door, so she dropped the book into her bag and closed the compartment just as Eduardo's secretary entered to escort her from the palace.

An old Lancia Delta belonging to Eduardo's cook was waiting at the curb. The cook's husband, a lout of a man who spoke no English, drove Fanny to Fiumicino Airport, where she and her luggage, which had been packed for her, were loaded onto a plane bound for Los Angeles.

Fanny had no idea how she'd get back to her mom's place from California. She also had no idea just what she'd taken from Eduardo, nor what he and his family would do when they found out it was missing. All she knew was that she desperately needed to make some money quickly when she got back to Los Angeles.

She would have to contact the Nolans.

# CHAPTER 2

Chicago, 1998.
*Lust is an itch that has to be scratched.*

Charley Brooks was feeling extremely optimistic. It was Friday afternoon and the meeting with the editor of *Hot Diets* had gone remarkably well. "Fuck Food, Eat Pussy," his parody on sex as an alternative to hamburgers, was just the kind of controversial article *Hot Diets* was looking for to distinguish it from its more conventional competitors catering to the latest fads for the obesity epidemic facing America.

"I love, love, love this," had gushed Barry Klinkhammer as he read through the text. "It's both tongue-in-cheek and tongue-in-you know where, if you know what I mean."

He winked at Charley, who knew exactly what he meant, though in reality it had been a long time since Charley'd had his tongue in anything but his own mouth.

"Hah, brilliant, Charley. We're going to run with this, my friend!"

He walked over to his desk and pulled a large checkbook from one of the drawers. Then he cut Charley a check for an amount that would keep him in a good deal of comfort for at least three months.

"I want to tell you, pal, anything you have involving food and sex, you just send it over. Man, you've got a knack for this stuff. And it's just the kind of shit—and I don't mean that in a bad way—that our readers lap up. Let me know if you need a research assistant and I'll 'arrange for one to work with you.' Very discreetly, of course." He'd made this last assurance in air quotes, though Charley missed the point entirely.

Klinkhammer was a short, thin, sweaty man. The few strands of ginger hair he had left on his head invariably fell over his right ear, making him look like a character from a Robert Crumb cartoon. He peered at Charley through his gold-rimmed glasses as he waited on a response to what he deemed a very generous offer.

"My articles are really more parody that factual, Barry. I mean, I can't imagine I'd need anyone to look stuff up for me."

"Not that kind of research. Jesus, what the hell do you think I'm talking about? I mean a researcher who'll help you with the subject matter. Get it?"

"I think I do," replied Charley, still not getting it at all, and realizing it was time to leave. "That's very kind of you, Barry, but I really prefer to do my own research. I hope you understand."

"Sure, Charley. Your loss, though. Let me know if you change your mind. It could help you with your next piece."

Charley had thanked him profusely and, looking at his watch, promised he'd think about Klinkhammer's offer as he said goodbye and walked out of the glass edifice on La Salle Street that housed Q10 Publications.

Now he had more than enough time to catch the 3:30 United flight back to New York and surprise his fiancée with a celebratory dinner at La Grenouile. It was almost dark outside, and, looking up, a raindrop of impressive proportions hit him in the eye as the storm that had been sweeping across Lake Michigan finally arrived. True to form, Charley, who had gotten used to traveling light during his war-correspondent days, had neither raincoat nor umbrella. Faced with either getting drenched while trying to grab a taxi or finding shelter from the deluge for a short while, he sprinted into a small convenience store.

The store was empty except for the proprietor, who was sitting behind the counter reading the *Chicago Sun-Times* and sucking on a mango. Charley nodded at him and wandered around the shop looking at everything he didn't need. Towards the back of the store, just past the racks of cheap wine, was a wall of magazines. The various publications were separated into categories by a black Perspex partition. There was the usual array of popular generic magazines and what were clearly, on closer examination, soft porn. Charley picked up a *People* magazine and began to flip through it.

"This is a store, not a library," yelled the proprietor, who'd been watching him.

"I know that, and I promise you I will buy something."

"You had very much better do that, and if you decide on anything from the back racks, you must ensure to keep your hands out your pockets."

"Jesus, what kind of person do you think I am?"

"I am, as you can discern from my circumstances, neither a mind-reader nor a psychiatrist, and so I have no idea what kind of person you are. What I don't want to see is you masturbating while you look at those magazines. You put your hand in your pocket and I'm going to mace you."

"Don't worry about that, I'm not interested in this sort of magazine I assure you." Charley sniffed indignantly, picking up a *Hustler* and waving it at the proprietor before returning it to the stack. It wasn't that he had an aversion to looking at literature of a more salacious nature. In fact, he'd had numerous articles published in *Playboy* and *Penthouse* over the years, not to mention the piece he'd just sold to *Hot Diets*–though that, as Klinkhammer had so rightly put it, was more burlesque than bawdy.

As Charley returned the *Hustler*, he noticed that the very back row housed magazines for the more erotically discerning. He looked over at the proprietor, who'd gone back to his mango and newspaper. Then, with the curiosity of both a male and a writer, and as with as subtle a movement as he could manage, Charley pulled aside the *Playboys*, *Hustlers* and *Penthouses* to get a proper gander at what lay before him. The magazines were equally split between ones that focused on large breasts and those that catered to men with a predilection for big backsides. Charley, had anyone asked him, would have said he was definitely more of a breast man, but no one had, and in truth when he did fantasize, the images were of women who were modestly proportioned, like his fiancée, whom he loved dearly and thought of as extremely sexy. Nevertheless, the writer in him demanded due diligence and so, having glossed over the breast section, he turned his gaze to the big-bottom magazines. Just as he was about to turn away, one caught his eye.

It wasn't so much the title–Porky Asses. *Big round meaty butts for the man who likes more than a handful*–that grabbed his attention, but the woman featured on the cover. She sat on a barstool, leaning forward so that her formidable buttocks jutted out in an extremely provocative way. 'Meet Fanny Packer,' read the subtitle, 'the woman who put the Ass in Class.'

He paused, staring at her, and then began to sweat profusely.

Charley, who'd once insulted a Bosnian warlord and drunk palm wine with a Congolese rebel who'd just lopped off the hands of a dozen prisoners, felt his knees go weak. Something distinctly odd was happening to him. He began to hyperventilate, and the blood rushed from his head. Much to his horror his penis began to harden, and in his panic he swung around, dislodging a bunch of magazines from the lower shelves. Try as he might he couldn't hide the bulge in his pants from the proprietor who, sensing something was up, walked over.

"Hey, hey, hey," he yelled, waving the remnants of his mango at Charley. "I knew you were up to no good. I'm going to have to mace you." He held up a rusty-looking canister and pointed it at Charley.

"Don't be ridiculous," shouted Charley, trying to cover both his eyes and the unruly tent in his pants. He grabbed *Porky Asses* and held it up. "I'll buy it, I'll buy it ... I'm a writer, I'm doing research."

"Do you know how many times I've heard that one?" It wasn't really a question. The proprietor took the magazine from Charley and, shaking his head, walked to the front, where he put it into a discreet brown paper bag.

"Sixty-five dollars."

"Are you crazy?"

"No, specialty magazines are expensive. And this one's a collector's item. Hot off the press. Now either give me the money or get out."

"Do you take credit cards?"

"Does this look like Barnes & Noble?"

Charley didn't argue. He couldn't. As much as he wanted to simply walk away, he knew that he had to find out more about Fanny Packer. The second he'd laid eyes on her, the emotional band that connected his heart to his head snapped. In all fairness to Charley, the sensation that defied reason entirely had as much to do with her face as her derriere. He was more than in love. He was well and truly smitten.

He took three twenties and a five from his wallet, paid the owner, and walked out clutching the paper bag to his chest. He wished to hell he'd brought a briefcase. The good news was it had stopped raining and there seemed to be plenty of taxis. He stuck out the arm not holding the bag and hailed one, hoping the driver took credit cards.

The traffic from downtown Chicago to O'Hare was still on the lighter side.

"We'll be there in about thirty-six minutes," said the driver in what Charley thought to be a strong Nigerian accent.

"Thanks, I'm just going to sit back here and read this magazine...."

"Don't worry, you don't have to talk to me. You're the passenger. It is your right not to have to talk. I will just focus on the traffic as I do ten hours a day and think about the horrors I have been through in my life."

"What? Sorry, did you say something?" Charley had been so focused on the first page of the magazine showing Fanny on all fours, her beautiful face smiling at him and her rear reflected provocatively in a mirror, that he hadn't really heard a word.

"Of course, like everyone you are deaf to the things that drove me from Nigeria to this unfriendly country."

"No, I'm not at all, but I really have to look at this magazine ... it's for research purposes," he added, hoping the driver would find it more believable than the proprietor of the convenience store. He held the magazine low so the driver couldn't see it in his mirror.

"Oh, really."

To Charley's horror, the driver turned around fully and took a quick glance at the cover, narrowly missing a large truck that was trying to change lanes.

"What the hell," yelled Charley as the momentum caused the magazine to fly from his hands onto the front seat.

"Oh, yes," said the driver as he picked up *Porky Asses*, which was now open to a page that featured an obese woman bent over to display cellulite-covered thighs and other intimate parts, and whose appeal could only have been to men interested in spelunking or forestry.

"Oh, yes," he repeated, flicking the pages as he wove through the traffic, "I can see why you want to research this. It is exactly to my taste. This is the type of woman I dreamed of at the detention camp while my comrades were being tortured. Do you mind if I take a look?"

"Yes, I do. I mind a great deal."

"Really? After all I've been through? Have you ever been tied over an anthill with your private parts covered in honey?"

"Not that I can recall. Jesus, look I'm sorry about your past, but buy your own … fuck, watch out." Another truck swung into their lane, and the driver, who was now steering with his knees, whether by divine intervention or sheer luck, narrowly avoided broadsiding it.

"I tell you what," said the driver as he again pulled the magazine away from Charley just as he'd managed to grab it back, "if you give this to me, I won't charge you for the trip."

"Absolutely not, I need that. It's mine. Now give it back it, you bastard."

"There is no need for name-calling."

"There absolutely is. There'll be need for cop-calling if you don't give it back immediately."

"Somehow, I doubt that. Hmm, I have to say this is a fantastic magazine. Take a look at this one. You could park a motorcycle between her buttocks." He flicked his eyes back to the road as an ambulance, its siren screaming, cut in front of him. It was the break Charley needed, and with one valiant effort he grabbed the magazine and pulled for all he was worth. To his absolute horror it tore in half, and he was left holding the first five pages.

"Now look what you've done. You've destroyed her. You've destroyed the woman I'm in love with." He could hardly believe what he'd just said. But it was all true, and he had no idea why. A great sadness swept through him and his eyes began to swell with tears, surprising both him and the driver. Then, through the mist, he looked at the pages clenched in his now quivering hand, and slowly stopped sniveling. He had retained the part that showed Fanny in all her glory. A gentle euphoria replaced the melancholy. She was mind-bogglingly beautiful. Neither fat nor porcine in the manner suggested by the title of the magazine. Large, yes. Voluptuous, certainly. And curvaceous in a way one might describe the grand staircase of a stately home. She had a profusion of red hair that fell gently across her shoulders, but did nothing to hide her face. Her skin was smooth and firm as a peach, and her green eyes were vulnerable yet strangely im-penetrable, and burned their way into Charley's head. But while her countenance alone would have been mesmerizing under normal circumstances, it did nothing to distract from the rest of her. Her breasts were indeed large, but they seemed devoid of silicone as they cavorted playfully above her smooth, concave belly. A flame-red pubic patch the size of a small doormat, and trimmed like freshly mown grass, pointed towards the next page that featured her gluteus amplificus. Charley studied Fanny's bottom and decided that whomever had coined the phrase, "put the ass in class," hadn't even begun to capture the sentiment's sublime magnificence. To his mind it defied any known adjectives.

His reverie was interrupted by the driver who, having seen desperate men before, offered Charley the other half of the magazine in a supreme act of sympathy.

"No," said Charley, "you keep it. This way we can both be happy."

"Your generosity is only exceeded by your good taste, sir. Now that will be twenty dollars without tip, and no I don't take credit cards."

They'd pulled up to Terminal One at O'Hare International Airport. Charley carefully folded the pages and put them in his jacket pocket. He pulled his last twenty from his wallet and handed it to the driver.

"You already have your tip."

"Well, I have half a tip but that's okay. I am happy to have met a fellow ass worshipper."

Charley, though hardly wishing to be included in this niche category of flesh worshippers, accepted the token of friendship humbly. He nodded a thank-you and walked into the United Terminal. Security was a breeze and his flight to New York was on time.

He had no idea what he'd say to Alexandra, his fiancé, but he was convinced their relationship was over.

# CHAPTER 3

In Charley's apartment and a hotel in New York. Same time.

*Relationships are relay races, in which only one person carries the baton.*

The taxi dropped him off at his apartment on 75th and Broadway. It was only 6:30, and he didn't expect Alexandra to be home for another two hours from her office on Third Avenue. She was an account director at a large advertising firm, and there was always some crisis that kept her working late. She'd get home frustrated, need to go to the gym to relax, and then want nothing more than a salad, a glass of wine, and to fall into bed and not have sex. Alexandra was thirty-four to Charley's forty, and he wondered—usually as he lay at least six inches from her in the bed when she was too hot to spoon—whether he was perhaps too old for her. Six years was a lifetime between someone who'd reported on war and brutality and someone who thought the waiter should be deported for forgetting to keep the onions off her salad. Then he'd fall asleep, and when he woke up in the morning he'd sigh in contentment as he looked at her lying next to him, perfectly formed, absolutely stunning with long dark straight hair and a nose that was the envy of everyone who hadn't managed to get an appointment with Dr. Myron Kahn, plastic surgeon to the wives and daughters of hedge fund managers.

Charley and Alexandra had met at the opening of a photography exhibition in Chelsea a year before. A number of the photos had been featured in stories Charley had reported on during a particularly brutal conflict in the Congo, and he was there to support his friend and ex-partner, the photographer, who was hoping the publicity from the show would help him transition into the world of commercial photography. Alexandra was there with her current boyfriend, an art director at her agency who was hoping to find an edgy new photographer for his next campaign.

Charley, after congratulating his friend and grabbing a limp shrimp from the hors d'oeuvres tray, was wandering around sipping on the awful box wine when he noticed the startlingly beautiful woman standing before one of the photographs. The shot in question was of a Congolese general, a skinned monkey draped over his head, the dripping hand of an enemy combatant he'd just dismembered held up for display. The woman had turned her head away in disgust while the man she was with just laughed.

"Oh, come on, Alex. You can't possibly believe this is real. It's all bullshit. Totally faked."

Charley, averse in general to conflict, shook his head and was about to walk away when something about the woman made him stop. He blinked his eyes and took a closer look. Her thick black hair was pulled back in a loose bun, accentuating her high cheekbones and delightful little nose. She was dressed in a tight white linen dress that came down to a few inches above her knees, revealing long slender legs that were finished off with a pair of flat black tennis shoes. There was nothing about her that was displeasing, other than the person she was with. To be fair, the instant dislike that Charley took to her companion had more to do with the fact that he'd decided that he was in love with his beautiful woman than it did the man's greasy hair, trendy black outfit, and arrogant opinions.

"Excuse me," he said, walking up to the pair. "Did I hear you say that this was faked?"

"Obviously," drawled the man, turning towards Charley with a look of total contempt on his face.

"You're wrong. This is real."

"I wouldn't argue with Mason," said the woman. "He's one of the top art directors in New York. If he says it's fake, it's fake."

Her companion rolled his eyes.

"It really isn't. I was there when he took this shot."

"Oh, bullshit, and do fuck off, please. We're busy."

"Wait, Mason. Let's listen to what he has to say." Alexandra was looking with interest at the big man with the disheveled hair. She noticed he wore his old dark-olive combat coat, unlike her male friends at Brown, as if he'd genuinely been in some dangerous places. His face was soft, almost helpless, she thought, but his eyes had depth and grit, as though he'd witnessed stuff she didn't necessarily want to think about.

"Oh, Jesus, Alexandra," said Mason. "Honestly, don't get taken in by this guy. I've met phonies like him before. Let's just go, I've seen enough to know this photographer has fuck-all chance of making it."

But something about the man intrigued Alexandra. "You go if you like, Mason. I want to hear what he says." And with that, Alexandra turned and stuck out her hand. "I'm Alexandra Cornell, and you are...?"

"Charley Brooks. I was a war correspondent in the Congo for *Time* magazine when Jeff took that shot."

"My God, you saw this guy cut off the hand?"

"I'm afraid I did, and a lot worse."

"Oh, please. No one does that sort of thing." Mason flicked his nose dismissively.

"Thomas Lubanga did. That was just after he cut out the liver of another soldier and ate it. He wanted me to have a bite, but I told him I'm not overly fond of organ meat."

"Now you're kidding...."

"No, I'm not. I'm serious. I hate organ meat." Charley laughed when he saw Alexandra's expression.

Mason uttered a rolling 'ugh' and walked off. Much to Charley's surprise, Alexandra gave Mason the finger behind his back and moved closer to Charley. "Didn't really like him anyway. I tell you what, why don't you take me to dinner and you can tell me all about it."

Their relationship began like no other Charley had ever experienced. It moved quickly, and within weeks they were living together, and Alexandra was throwing dinner parties for all her friends and family to meet Charley. The transition from his life in various war zones around the world—which had been Spartan at best—to Alexandra's world, wasn't easy for Charley. They were the same sort of surroundings and people he'd grown up with in Connecticut, and the very reason he moved away, and thrown himself into a lifestyle that was as far from Greenwich as he could possibly get. Yet here he was, back in the thick of it. There were times he'd felt himself drowning and others when he believed he was where he should be. She'd only once asked about his parents, and on learning they were dead, left it at that. Far from being hurt by her lack of interest in his background, Charley was relieved. He had no desire to talk about what had happened and how profoundly it had affected him.

As the months progressed, he began to think more and more about what a friend of his, a successful clinical psychologist, had told him over a few beers one night. "People start and end relationships for the same reason. We start them because the other person is so different, and we end them because the other person is so different. You can't be what you're not, Charley. You can pretend for a while, but pretense is not a long-term proposition."

Charley worried about this a lot at night, but he stopped in the mornings. He desperately wanted a relationship, and Alexandra had been his only current option. So the wedding was planned for the end of August at Alexandra's parents' estate in East Hampton, and the one thing Charley dreaded more than telling Alexandra that he was suddenly in love with someone else was what her father would say when he realized he'd be cancelling the whole she-bang. Come to think of it, Charley consoled himself, he'd probably be thrilled. "That guy wasn't right for you, Alexandra. Never was in my opinion." Well, that's what he'd implied when she'd first introduced Charley to him. Alexandra's father was a relatively percep-tive man.

Alone in the apartment, Charley carefully took out the folded pages from his jacket pocket. Just as he was about to open them, he found himself looking at a picture of Alexandra he had taken on the beach in East Hampton. He picked it up and examined his stunning fiancée in her string bikini and aviator sun-glasses, and suddenly the current madness of his de-sire began to wane. Perhaps a quick look at the pic-tures of Fanny would bring him back to reality and he'd be able to destroy them. Of course, that was it. He'd look and laugh and chide himself for his stupid behavior. He's never been turned on by large women before. It had been one crazy moment. It would di-sappear with one brief look.

But it didn't. As he once again devoured Fanny in all her glory, his pulse began to race anew, and his penis, flaccid since La Guardia, sprung to attention. It writhed around his boxers like an Indian cobra im-patiently waiting for its charmer, and right then and there he simply gave up.

Charley's uncontrollable reverie was interrupted by a giggling sound that came from outside the apartment door. Lust gave way to sheer panic as he realized it was Alexandra. If she caught him with his penis out and the large-lady pages, he'd be the laughing stock of all their friends.

With the agility of a man who'd been in tight corners before, Charley pulled up his pants and shoved the pages under one of the cushions on the couch. He stood up just as Alexandra skipped in looking over her shoulder at a tall individual who made a grab at her. She giggled even harder before turning to see Charley for the first time.

"Charley, oh my God...."

Charley immediately looked down. His guilt forced him to assume that she knew what he was up to. But both the pages and his penis were safely out of sight, and he quickly looked up again just as Alexandra evaded another grab.

"What are you doing home so early, darling? I wasn't expecting you for an hour. Oh, stop, Howard. Can't you see Charley's here...." She giggled again.

It was the opening that Charley needed.

"I had some good news. I wanted to surprise you and it looks like I did. You can come on out from behind her, Howard. I'm not going to punch your fucking lights out. Although I certainly feel like it."

Howard, their neighbor from across the hall, wasn't sure he quite believed Charley, who had balled his substantial hands into even more substantial fists.

"Don't you dare hit me, Charley," Howard yelped. "I've got a weak heart."

"You have a weak everything, you piece of crap. You're a damn coward, doing things behind my back."

"Oh, come on, Charley," said Alexandra, smoothing her hair. "You're always so dramatic. Jesus!!! Howard and I were just having some fun. He was showing me his latest idea that's going to make him millions."

"It's sculpt-by-numbers," replied the recovering Howard, going into full salesman mold. "People get a full block of white plaster delivered with carefully designed and marked numbered pieces and then they just chip away until a nymph or rampant bull appears. It's quite genius."

Charley softened for a second, until he noticed the while plaster handprints around the thigh and breast area of Alexandra's black jumpsuit.

"Ah, and let me guess, you needed to make sure you had the right proportions for the nymph by fondling Alex?"

Alexandra tried to assuage the situation by kissing Charley on the cheek, and Howard saw the perfect opening to slink out.

But assuaging was not what Charley needed. Evidence of Alexandra's infidelity presented an opportunity that was too good to pass up.

"Look, Alex...."

"I hate it when you call me that."

"I'm sorry—Alexandra, then. This is hard to say...."

Alexandra recoiled from him. Her face, despite a heavy application of makeup, was ashen.

"But," continued Charley, "I don't think we should be together anymore."

Alexandra said nothing for a few seconds, and then the blood that had vacated her face for parts unknown returned with a vengeance. "You fucking bastard. Just because I was having some fun with Howard?"

"No, it's not just that. We're, uh, just different people." It was the best Charley could come up with under the circumstances.

"That's it? You only just discovered we're different people and so you want to leave? After nearly a year? After my father has planned this huge wedding? After all the great sex I gave you? After I let you do that thing the other night?"

"What thing? Whatever it was, it wasn't me. We really haven't had sex for months. You've been too tired."

"You're not just an idiot, Charley, you're delusional. What? Have you found someone else?"

"No...." That part at least was true. He hadn't actually found Fanny yet, and he wasn't even sure how he'd go about it.

# CHAPTER 4

Rome, a few days before.
*A hit man is no match for a hitman.*

Eduardo had waited two weeks to tell his uncle, the present Marchese di Custoza, about the missing book. His uncle, normally a nasty man, was incensed. Slightly more so than Eduardo had envisaged. He knew this because the marchese's face, normally red from copious quantities of grappa and wine, had turned an alarming shade of purple.

The marchese stood up from behind his desk and strode with a fierce determination to where Eduardo stood, strategically positioned close to the door. "You waited how long before you decided to tell me that this fat putana had stolen our book?"

"Just two weeks, Uncle Bruno. But I had good reasons. And just for your, um, information, she was actually a belly dancer, not a prostitute, which I know is quite amusing." He laughed.

By this point the marchese had reached Eduardo and without saying a word, he slapped his nephew viciously across the face. The blow was so hard that

Eduardo toppled over into the doorframe, where he looked up at his uncle with slightly glazed eyes.

"Get up, you fool, I want to hit you again...."

Eduardo's mouth was thick with blood. He couldn't open it, but even if he could have, he realized that saying nothing was the safest thing to do. He certainly didn't want to stand up and be hit again, so he slid down even further into a fetal position.

"Very well, then, I will have to kick you." The marchese, who would have been classified as a heavy-weight contender had he been forty years younger and eighty kilograms lighter, tried to lift his leg to kick his nephew. After a few attempts and nearly falling over, he turned around and stomped back to his desk, shaking his head in disgust. He snarled at Eduardo, who still hadn't stood up.

Bruno Adamo Christoforo Sabatini, fifth Marchese di Custoza, hated his nephew with an almost insane passion. If he hadn't believed somewhat in the Virgin Mary, and that the promise he'd made his older brother, Eduardo's father, Desiderio, as he lay dying, was sacrosanct, he would have killed Eduardo years ago. He thought back to that fateful day when he'd sworn the oath. It was the day after the assassin he'd hired from the Camorra in Naples had killed his sister-in-law. The idiot hitman had failed, despite firing six bullets, to kill the real target, his brother, who instead had been left desperately clinging to the last vestiges of his time on earth in an intensive care unit in one of Rome's better private hospitals. Bruno had booted the priest out of his brother's room just as he'd been about to administer the Last Rites, so he could get in a few final requests to the titular head of the family. But Desiderio got in first.

"I want you to promise me, Bruno, on the soul of our father whom I will shortly see, that you will protect and raise my son as if he was your own."

"But I hate the little bastard."

"Well, no one really likes him, Bruno. He is a little odd, I know. But he is my son, your nephew. And he will be the one to ensure that our family survives for eternity."

"Are you sure, Desiderio? I mean I really should be the one. I'm extremely virile for a man my age, and quite frankly we don't even know whether Eduardo will grow up liking women. He seems a little fruity, if you know what I mean."

"Then introduce him to Bella Castiglione when he turns sixteen. She will fuck the fanook out of him." The fourth marchese coughed up a large gob of blood. "For Christ's sake, Bruno, I'm dying. Please do this for me. He will inherit the book when he turns twenty-one. That is final. I cannot give it to you. And where is the damn priest?"

"I'll get him in one minute. In the meantime, what do I get?"

"What do you mean 'What do I get?' You have control of the family."

"I think you need to sweeten the deal. I'm not really buying this 'look after my son' thing."

"You must swear this oath, Bruno. Now I'm going fast, and I'm too weak to argue. Take the title if you want it. Take the bigger palazzo if it makes you happy, and put Eduardo in the Arcieri with a governess. Now swear to me...."

"Fine, I swear on our father's soul, but I think I you should reconsider the book.... Hey, wake up!" It was too late for Bruno to demand more. His brother's eyes rolled back and he gasped his last breath.

At that moment, the priest rushed back in. "Don't tell me...."

"I was just about to get you, Father. I think maybe he's sleeping."

"No, he's dead, you idiot. And now he's condemned to eternal hell ... and it's entirely your fault."

"Really? Hmm, well don't expect me to feel too bad for him. I am going to go through hell too looking after his stupid son."

Most men would have been satisfied with the power and the money and the title. But not Bruno. He was a dolt, a thug, an ingrate, and his avarice was overwhelming. As the years went by and his virility waned, his desire for the book and everything it was purported to do became an obsession. But he couldn't touch it. Not yet. Not while his nephew lived. It was time to arrange for an accident.

"You are useless, useless, Eduardo. If I hadn't promised your father that I would look after you, I would have your throat slit. Now, I am a generous man, so I'm going to give you one more opportunity to recover the book."

"Thank you, Uncle. I won't let you down."

"Yes, you will. And that is why someone will accompany you."

"Of course, Uncle Bruno. I will ask Marco Pacchini. He is, as you know, my best man."

"I don't give a shit if he is your best man. You will take my best man." The Marchese pushed a button on his desk and the door behind Eduardo opened.

From Eduardo's vantage, it seemed as if an apelike creature had walked into the room. Then as Eduardo slowly rose to his feet, he saw that it was in fact a monstrous dwarf. He was dressed in grey pants, an extremely tight black jacket. A porkpie hat, possibly a few sizes too small, was perched on his misshapen head. The homunculus was as wide as he was tall, and his arms came down to his knees. Eduardo had never met Nano Mortale before, but he knew of his awesome reputation, and he was terrified.

"Nano Mortale," said the marchese, "this is my useless nephew, Eduardo. You will accompany him to America, where you will find that big belly dancer, and you will get the book from her. After you have done that you will kill her in your usual fashion, and if my nephew stands in your way at any point, then kill him too. You can make his death painless. He is family, after all."

The marchese laughed, but the dwarf just grunted.

# CHAPTER 5

New York, later that same day.

*Never underestimate the power of a large martini or two.*

Back at the apartment, things had gone from awful to horrific. Alexandra had raged at Charley for the first ten minutes. Then she'd cried in distress. Huge tears filled her eyes and a good deal of snot hung from her nose. While the crying almost broke Charley's heart, he managed to summon the resolve that had once got him through a negotiation with a Shining Path guerrilla leader pointing a .357 magnum revolver at him, and held his ground. Finally she spat in his face, which, while it shocked him, he believed was deserved.

"I want you out of this apartment in five minutes."

"But Alexandra, it's my apartment...."

She scowled at him and stormed out of the room, leaving Charley with the suspicion that his ownership of the apartment had become a minor and completely irrelevant detail. Deciding that he could probably sort it all out later, Charley retrieved the remnants of *Porky Asses* from its hiding place and hastily packed a suitcase. On his way to the elevator he called up a midtown hotel and booked a room for a couple of days. While not fancy, it had a fairly decent bar and would be adequate for the task to which he intended to dedicate himself.

There had to be a way to find Fanny, he was convinced of that. He just didn't know what that way was. His first thought while checking into the hotel was to see who the publisher of *Porky Asses* was, but the cab driver had ended up with both the back and front covers and there were no words on the pages so lovingly stuffed into his jacket pocket above his heart. In his room, he sat on the bed and stared at a painting on the wall, a landscape that looked to be either in ancient Japan or a place from *Grimms' Fairy Tales* populated by evil imps. After a few seconds, he concluded that everything would become a distraction unless he cleared his head and focused on the job at hand.

He reached into his pocket and took out the pages that were now beginning to show signs of wear on the hastily applied folds. He flattened them as best he could and gazed lovingly at the woman who had inserted herself into his psyche, capturing his heart and kindred organs so dramatically and with such cataclysmic consequences. He scanned each page carefully, desperately trying not to be diverted by the lure of breast, buttocks or face, but there was no clue whatsoever. He would have to return to Chicago to pay another visit to the convenience store tomorrow, as he was definitely too exhausted to do it now, and in any case was hungry and needed a martini.

He went down to the hotel bar, ordered a very dry gin martini and a hamburger, and tried to focus his thoughts. He'd been in situations that were life-threatening, but never ones that would qualify as life-changing. This was different, and he was scared. Suddenly he found his mind drawn to another bar, in another time, ten thousand miles from New York.

Charley's throat had been parched from the dust kicked up by his Land Cruiser on the endless dirt road between Francistown and Maun, the tiny Botswanan oasis that lay at the gateway to one of the greatest wildlife areas in the world; the Okavango Swamps. Even more, the midday temperature had been hovering around the 100-degree mark on the old rusty thermometer nailed to a beam on the veranda of the Duck Inn. Under these conditions, the cold beer, the first cool drink he'd had in two days, had barely seemed to touch the sides of his throat as he drained the bottle in one gulp.

Charley was in Africa for a very specific purpose: to interview the legendary guerrilla leader, Joe Kamerera, who was hiding out in Botswana to plan his next raid into what was then white-controlled Rhodesia. Getting Kamerera to agree to see him and trying to arrange times without the ability to communicate by telephone or radio had been an absolute nightmare. All arrangements—and they'd been vague at best—had been through journalist friends in Botswana with connections to the guerrillas. But *Playboy* was paying him well for the interview, and covering all expenses.

"Charles Brooks?"

Charley looked around in surprise. The voice belonged to an old man in torn army fatigues who'd somehow managed to walk up to his table without Charley seeing him.

"Yes...."

"You are to come with me, please."

"Are you with Commander Kamerera?"

"Just follow me please, sir. And do not ask any more questions or everything you are here for is off."

Charley, his heart thumping against his rib cage in both fear and excitement, stood up, threw a few notes on the table, and followed the old soldier to his Land Cruiser, where another younger man stood holding a battered AK-47.

"Hand me the keys, please," said the older man.

"No way. It's not insured for someone else to drive it."

"Mr. Brooks," said the soldier, shaking his head. "For a famous journalist, you are a fool. Do you seriously believe that we would allow you to see where we are going?"

"Well...."

"There is no 'well.' Here's how it works. I will drive you to our camp while you lie on the backseat with this bag over your head. My comrade here will have his gun pointed at you the whole journey. If you talk at any time or try to see where we are going, he will kill you. Is that clear?"

Charley gulped. "Perfectly."

He handed over the keys and got in the back. As the younger man put the bag over his head, Charley felt his first surge of panic. The bag had been used for corn meal, and every time he breathed he inhaled enough of it to turn his lungs into two giant taco shells.

"I can't breathe."

"Yes, you can. Just don't take deep breaths. We are not trying to kill you. Not yet, anyway."

He bounced around like a jellyfish in a coffee grinder as the Land Cruiser made its way through the thick sand and over the inevitable corrugations that turned bush roads into bone-crunching paths through hell. Thorn bushes scraped and broke along the sides and undercarriage, and Charley knew they must have turned off into the deep bush. He was going into the true unknown, with no one to get him out if things got rough. As an American journalist, he felt reasonably confident that no one would murder him indiscriminately, but out here he was just another white man caught up in a conflict designed specifically to get rid of white people. He cursed his ridiculous desire to take on the assignment mostly to prove his manliness to his current girlfriend, whose brothers had both been Rangers in Vietnam.

After what seemed like an eternity the Land Cruiser came to a stop, and the younger soldier pulled the sack off Charley's head. He sat up and looked out the window. The bush was dense but it was still light enough for him make out a few huts and tents scattered around a clearing in which men and women in military fatigues were sitting round a large fire.

As Charley got out of the Land Cruiser, a man emerged from the nearest hut. Joe Kamerera could not have been more than five feet three inches tall, but his smile seemed as broad as his shoulders.

"Ah, Mr. Charles Brooks, the well-known journalist who has come all this way to hear my story. Welcome to our little home. If you need to pee, as I imagine you do, please use my private bathroom. It's that tree over there."

What Joe may have lacked in height he more than made up for with a smile as broad as his shoulders. He took Charley's hand and shook it vigorously.

"Come and sit round our fire and meet some of my comrades. Our story, as you will hear, is as much ours as it is the story of all Africans since the white man came to take our land."

There were fifty-three freedom fighters in the camp. Some were veterans of many battles and others young men and women who'd never held a gun before they joined Kamerera's unit. They stared at Charley with a mixture of hatred and suspicion, and he felt extremely unnerved as he sat on the hard ground eating from a communal bowl of hard corn porridge.

"You have to understand my people, Charles. Their only encounters with the white man have not been pleasant. In fact, exactly the opposite. The whites came and took our land and our cattle. Then they took whatever else they wanted and when we complained they took our limbs and our lives. It's time to give it back."

"And when you take it back, what will you do?"

"We will burn the whites and kill them and use their blood and bones to fertilize the soil," answered one of the others, a man with a large scar that stretched from his forehead to his chin.

"No, Robert," Joe said. "We will not do that. We are not the savages that they make us out to be." He turned back to Charley. "I'm sorry, Charles. You must forgive comrades like Robert here. He was caught and beaten by a unit of the Selous Scouts and left for dead in the bush. It's hard for him to understand our objective."

"What is your objective?"

"When we take over, and that is only a matter of time, we will ask the whites to share the land—in proportion, of course—and we will work with them to make Zimbabwe, as it will be called, one of the greatest countries in Africa."

"And if they don't?"

"Then we will ask them to leave in peace. But if they refuse, then I'm afraid my words will be as nothing to the anger of the young soldiers. But enough, you must be tired. We will talk more tomorrow."

Most of the troops had no time or desire to talk to Charley, but Joe gave him as much time as he could in between training the younger soldiers and planning his next raid across the border. Charley wasn't permitted to take photos, but Joe answered most of his questions about his life as a freedom fighter and the horrors of colonialism and the havoc it had left behind. On the third day, Charley asked Joe the question that both changed, and very nearly cost him, his life.

"Are you ever afraid, Joe?"

"Of what, Charley? What should I be afraid of?"

"Well, of being caught and tortured and killed?"

"Yes, I am very much afraid of those things. What man would not be?"

"Do you want me to say that in the article? Surely not...?"

"You must write it. People must understand that our passion for the ideal transcends our fear of the physical. If you understand what your goal is, and you want it more than life itself, then anything that stands between you and it is irrelevant, and must be ignored if you are to succeed. Do you understand that?"

"I guess so. I mean, it's a pretty lofty thought."

"It is, but not everything can be solved with the naïve and simple. Much of what is truth lies in complexity. This I have learned out here in the bush the hard way. Now let me ask you a question, Charley: are you afraid right now?

"Not right now...."

"You should be. I could have you killed if I wanted to, or we could get bombed at any moment. But I tell you what, you have as much as you need from me for a good story. I would like to give you something extra. Let's call it a gift."

"What's that?"

"I would like to teach you to use your fear the way I've learned to use mine."

"Any how would we go about that?"

Joe asked Charley to accompany them the next morning as they crossed into Rhodesia, and after spending a good deal of the night quaking in terror at the thought of being ambushed, Charley finally decided to do it. He trusted Joe's gut feeling that they'd be perfectly safe on their recruitment drive into the deep Rhodesian bush.

It turned out to be a very valuable lesson indeed. Not so much on harnessing fear as never trusting the gut feeling of a lunatic idealist. They encountered a unit of the Rhodesian army just two hours after crossing the border, and the entire guerrilla force, including Joe, was wiped out. The only thing that saved Charley was his white skin and quick thinking. The Rhodesians, while they took no prisoners, believed him when he told them he'd been forced to participate in the Kamerera raid at gunpoint.

He never felt like a coward for screaming, "Don't shoot, I'm an American," at the young Rhodesian soldier who had the barrel of a Heckler & Koch G3 rifle jammed into his ear. The interview with Joe Kamerera that appeared in the September issue of *Playboy* that year was a tremendous hit for Charley, and set him up as a sought-after war correspondent for a number of news groups.

"Would you like another martini?"

Charley snapped out of his reverie. "Huh?"

The bartender, a young woman with long brown hair and emerald eyes, tapped his empty glass. "I said would you like another martini? This one seems to have evaporated into the same space you were just in."

Charley had no recollection of finishing his drink, but he could feel the effects. He worried a second one would dull his thinking even more, but ordered it anyway.

"Yes, please. Sorry I was on another planet."

"Everything okay?" She gave the cocktail shaker a vigorous jiggle.

"Not really, but it's complicated." He immediately regretted engaging her. He was in too delicate an emotional state, and the last thing he needed was someone else thinking he was weird.

"Well, if you want to talk, it's pretty empty and we don't get busy for another hour. I'm Gabriella, but you can call me Gaby."

"I'm Charley. Nice to meet you, Gaby." He shook her hand. "It's an odd problem I suppose. Quite a delicate one really. You see, I'm desperately trying to find a woman."

"Jesus." She picked up a bar towel and wiped her hand as if Charley had contaminated it.

"No, God no." Charley jumped up. "I'm sorry that came out wrong. That's not a pickup line either, I promise. I'm trying to find a particular woman and I don't know how to get her address."

Gaby looked at him as if she weren't quite sure she believed him. Charley paused. If he actually told her the real story, she'd most likely hit him with a bottle.

"Umm, look. She's someone I met long ago and I saw a picture of her in a magazine in Chicago earlier today, but I haven't a clue how to go about getting her contact info. That's it, I swear."

"Okay, okay, I think believe you. You don't look like a perv."

"Well, I'm certainly not," Charley said, though in the broadest sense of the word, he probably was one.

"So tell me the whole thing and let's take it from there." Gaby strained his martini into a large frosted glass, added a couple of olives, and slid it across to him. The fifteen seconds it took gave Charley the time he needed to get his story into some semblance of order.

"I was in Chicago this morning for a meeting. It was pouring rain when I finished, so I ran into a little convenience store and picked up a magazine to wait it out before grabbing a cab for the airport." So far, he thought, what he had said was all true, but the trickier part was yet to come. "It was one of those popular magazines with social pages, and I saw a woman that I knew a long time ago."

"Ah," Gaby pursed her lips as if she understood perfectly. "And you were in love with her back then."

"I guess I was, but I probably didn't know quite how much until I saw her in the magazine this morning. Then I left it in the cab." Charley closed his eyes and pictured Fanny's face. He must have looked sad and pathetic, because Gaby stroked his cheek.

"Ah, that's so sweet. I have to say, though, the answer seems quite obvious. Just find a newsstand—there's one in the lobby—and look for the magazine? I'm sure they'll have it."

"No, they absolutely won't." Charley took a hefty swig of the martini.

"You seem pretty certain."

"No, it's quite specialized. They won't have it."

"I thought you said it was popular?"

"It is, it is." The martini was kicking in and Charley was getting more befuddled by the second. "It's very popular among certain people. That's what I meant to say."

"You're not making much sense. What sort of magazine are you talking about?"

Charley tried desperately to think how he could describe *Porky Asses* without actually admitting anything. He briefly thought about talking about pigs and animal husbandry but immediately felt that would be a betrayal of Fanny.

"It's a diet magazine. For people who don't really want to lose weight. You know, people who feel great the way they are." It sounded desperate.

"You mean fat people? So you're looking for a fat woman?"

"Not exactly fat, more on the plus side. Big but not bulging in any way." Visions of Fanny swam before his eyes. "I mean she has very generous breasts...." As he said "breasts," he realized he should never have had the second martini.

"You know what, you do look like a perv and I'm sorry I even asked. Yuck." With that, Gaby walked away to take care of someone who'd just sat down at the other end of the bar.

Charley put his head in his hands. He knew that he was in a dangerous place. His obsession with finding Fanny had taken him to the edge of a precipice from which there was no turning back. He stared into the remains of his martini as if it was a crystal ball. And then and there, in the thick fog of his uncertainty and the last vestiges of five parts gin to one part vermouth, he suddenly knew what to do. He pulled out his flip phone and called Barry Klinkhammer, who surprisingly enough was still in his office in Chicago.

"Let me make sure I understand this, Charley. You want me to find out who publishes a magazine called *Porky Asses?*"

"Yes, please. I have an idea for you guys, but I need to interview someone who's featured in their latest publication."

"A diet for people with big asses? You're not drunk, are you?"

Charley was about to say he was, but Barry had already jumped back in.

"Know what, Charley, who cares? I like it. You're on a roll with diets and sex, man. I'll get our research people on it first thing in the morning and get back to you. Pussy, asses ... you're exploring things no one has touched before. Well, not in the way you're touching them."

Charley couldn't argue with anything Barry was saying. He was certainly drunk, and he was definitely delving into terra incognita. But he couldn't have stopped if he had wanted to. The little piece of the universe into which he'd inadvertently tumbled was moving faster than anything he'd ever experienced. He didn't have a clue as to where it would take him, and he didn't care. All he knew was that the joy was almost overwhelming. And the rapture was still to come.

By ten thirty the next morning Charley had his answer: Nolan Publication in Los Angeles. Equipped

with a phone number and address, he was on a plane
headed for LAX by 1:30.

# CHAPTER 6

In Los Angeles around the same time.
*Loneliness is having something to say but no one to say it to.*

"It's too late, darlin'. The magazine went live three days ago."

Fanny regarded Junior Nolan bleakly. "It can't possibly be too late, Mr. Nolan. Surely you can recall it. It can't have gone to that many places."

"Well, that may be true under normal circumstances, but to be honest, Fanny, in all my years in the business I've never seen a publication better received by our distributors. The last one that got a similar reaction was 'I Dream of Creamy, starring Honey Thize, the lady with the Hurrah in her Bra.' I wrote that line, too. Nearly as good as 'put the ass in class,' don't you think?

"It is very good, Mr. Nolan but...."

"Now, now, Fanny. I can see you're upset, and you know I'd do anything in the world to help you...." Junior Nolan stood up and walked around his large wooden desk to where Fanny sat slumped in her chair. He barely came up to the top of her ear. "But there's not a damn thing I can do in this case. It's just too late."

Fanny looked up and smiled. It was one of those rather sad and pathetic smiles that women are able to produce at will and most men are incapable of resisting. Junior Nolan was copresident with his wife Noleen of one of the largest publishers of specialty porn magazines in the US, and therefore could not be numbered in the ranks of 'most men.' He was, however, not entirely devoid of empathy, and the women whose attributes and appendages he so blatantly exploited, when in emotional distress, brought out whatever small amount of decency lay buried in his dark and decrepit eighty-four-year-old soul.

"Fanny," he said, putting his arms around her, "don't fret about this. First, you're one of the most beautiful gals I've ever had the pleasure and privilege of putting in one of my magazines. Honestly, Sunshine, you'd be as pretty as a peach if a peach was a big as a watermelon, and no man, no real man, would think anything badly about you. Second, there are only five hundred of those magazines in circulation. Yes that, and of course you, are what puts the 'special' in specialty. Another one of my lines by the way. So the odds of anyone you know and cherish seeing one is about as low as a hen winning the derby. There, feel better?"

Fanny looked up at Junior. His wizened features, reminiscent of a prune, made it hard to tell whether he was being genuine or not, but the slight sparkle in his rheumy eyes made her feel that he probably was.

"Thank you, Mr. Nolan. I honestly do feel better," she lied. "You were extremely generous, and I really need that money to get home to see my mom."

"You're very welcome, Fanny. And the money will be in your bank account in three days. Sorry we can't do cash. IRS bastards will have my balls for bear bait if I did that again. But here...," he said, taking fifty dollars from a wallet that was as gnarled as he was, "I'd hate to see you go hungry, a big gal like yourself."

"Oh, no, Mr. Nolan. I couldn't take it."

"Of course you can, Fanny. Not another word now."

"Well, thank you. I really appreciate it."

"Now off you go, and remember, Nolan Publications always has a need for women with your superb assets." He patted Fanny's behind as if to reinforce the point.

Two days later, Fanny had barely twenty dollars left in her purse. She sat in the spare bedroom of the Hollywood bungalow of her new friend Paula, who she'd met while waiting to do her shoot for *Porky Asses*. Paula had just finished the cover shot for her new magazine and offered to do Fanny's makeup, seeing as the Nolans were too cheap to pay for a proper makeup artist, and though they had little in common other than posing for magazines of questionable taste, the two hit it off immediately. After Paula heard what had happened to Fanny, she told her precisely what she'd have done to Eduardo had she been in Fanny's situation and offered Fanny a place to stay until her next check cleared and she could buy a bus ticket to get to Worland.

Paula was presently in her basement treating one of her patients, and judging by the yells emanating from behind the closed door, doing a superb job. The squeals didn't bother Fanny in the least. She'd grown up around women who were experts in treating men with certain disorders, and though she wasn't sure she fully understood exactly what it was that made men like that tick, she believed in the old adage of *whatever floats your boat.*

The problem was that nothing was floating Fanny's boat at the moment, and she couldn't quite work out why. She knew she loved belly dancing and she was confident that she was exceptionally good at it, but she was lonely and had been ever since she'd moved to Los Angeles. She liked Paula. The little she knew about her. But Paula didn't have time for whiners. And Fanny needed to whine.

After Fanny first graduated from the Los Angeles School of Belly Dancing with an advanced degree in Hip to Breast Transition, she had danced regularly at upscale Hollywood clubs and various events. Once, after a particularly stunning performance at a party hosted by George Lucas, the famous director had offered her a part in one of his *Star Wars* movies, dancing in a new version of the Chalmun's Cantina in the pirate city of Mos Eisley. She very politely declined. Belly dancing was serious business and not something she believed should be trivialized in any way.

It was also however, not something that paid overly well, and what money she made after her agent took his commission barely covered her rent, food, and membership at a West Hollywood gym. So when her agent told her about the job dancing at a palace in Rome, for a very distinguished client and an amount of money that was more than she could possibly make in a year, she couldn't contain her excitement. She immediately called up her mom to tell her the news.

"I don't like it, Fanny. I don't like it at all, sweetpea. Those sorts of jobs are fishier than last week's laundry. How much do you know about this Sabatini fella? Nothing, I'll bet. Sounds like pond scum to me. If you need money darlin', I'll send you whatever you want."

"No, Momma. I told you I don't want to take money from you. If I'm going to be a success, I need to do it on my own. In any case I have a very good feeling about this job. Even if it isn't any good, I'll be going on an all-expenses paid trip to Rome. And how amazing is that? Think of it, Italy.... Maybe I can even visit Florence or Venice and see some of those paintings. The Botticellis and Rubens, where you said the women always reminded you of me."

Her mother's concern gradually eased as she heard the enthusiasm in her daughter's voice. Fanny hadn't sounded this excited since she'd left Worland three years before to become a belly dancer, and hopefully to find her father. She'd certainly found her calling as a belly dancer, but of her father, there was no trace. Dreams do not obey the same universal laws as logic, and while deep down Fanny was too smart to believe that she would ever get to meet him, she had even consulted a young psychic named Milton Cayce, who claimed to be the great-great grandson of the famous Christian mystic, Edgar Cayce, and lived in a two-floor walk-up in Venice, California. He told Fanny that her father did not reside on this earth, but lived somewhere on a mountain in an entirely different world. He offered to take her there if she stripped entirely and accompanied him to his bedroom where he would ritually cleanse her for the trip. Fanny punched him in the face, took back her forty dollars, and vowed never to look for her father again.

She was busy massaging her forehead and chiding herself for thinking about the past and not focusing on what she was going to do when she got back to Worland when Paula, who'd just seen her client out the door, walked in.

"God, I hate it when my patients use their safe words before I've even warmed up. He wasn't even bleeding. It seems like such a waste of money when you think about it. I mean, why go to a doctor when you can diagnose yourself?"

Fanny wasn't sure the metapho worked but she was too upset to bring it up.

"Anyway," said Paula, lighting up a joint, "I've got an extra half-an-hour to sit and talk to you. So tell me, Fanny, why so damn glum?"

"Oh, Paula, you've been nice enough letting me stay here for a few days. You don't need to know my problems."

"Fanny," said Paula, sounding more like a teacher (which in fact was the role she'd just been playing), "I don't. But if you keep them to a minimum, I'll be glad to help. Now, tell me what's worrying you."

"Well, if you don't mind, I could definitely use some friendly advice."

Paula handed her the joint. "Here, take a puff ... and no, I don't mind at all. That's what I do. Although I doubt if any of my patients would claim it's 'friendly.'"

# CHAPTER 7

On a different plane between Rome and Los Angeles, same timeframe.
*Why short men don't tell tall tales.*

Eduardo Sabatini wasn't happy. He was still smarting from his uncle's rebuke, and the dwarf was not a great travel companion. To start, he'd insisted on the aisle seat when clearly the window seat would have been a more considerate choice for someone whose legs occupied greater width than depth. Because Nano's big feet stuck out over the seat, it made it hard for Eduardo, who had a weak bladder and needed to visit the bathroom often, to squeeze by. Nano had also drunk a copious amount of the free vodka available in Business Class and was terrifying the other passengers with a hideous scowl every time they looked at him.

"So Nano," said Eduardo, trying desperately to be friendly in case a closer relationship would help if the mission was unsuccessful, "what is your favorite manner of killing? The one my uncle mentioned."

The dwarf grunted something between mouthfuls of the lasagna that the flight attendant had just put down in front of him.

"I'm sorry," said Eduardo, "I didn't quite catch that."

Nano gave an even more incomprehensible grunt.

"Well, I hope I personally never have to experience it, and my uncle was clear with you on that subject, but I am very interested in killing methods. You know I did a fair amount when I worked with the Chicago outfit."

Nano grabbed an orange from the fresh fruit tray the flight attendant was carrying down the aisle, and squeezed it till it exploded like a grenade, showering the passengers in front and to the side with pulp and juice.

"Madonna," whispered Eduardo. "You squeeze their heads until they explode. How ingenious." The passenger in the seat in front of Nano, who'd been wanting to say something to the parent of what he assumed was a badly behaved child behind him kicking the back of his seat, shot up in anger and yelled at Eduardo.

"Hey, can't you control your brat?"

Eduardo stared at him as if the man was mad. Anyone who mistook Nano Mortale for a child was either blind or off his rocker. Much to Eduardo's surprise, Nano remained calm for a second or two. Then he climbed up onto the seat and grabbed the angry passenger's upper lip and began to twist it. The man could neither talk nor scream. Nano leaned over the backrest and dragged the unfortunate passenger's head till it was six inches from the armrest. Then he smashed it down with such force that the man slumped back into his seat, either unconscious or dead. Eduardo didn't want to know which.

The dwarf sat back down as if nothing had happened and indicated that he wanted another vodka to the flight attendant, who pretended not to notice the potential corpse.

"I'm afraid my methods are more conventional," Eduardo lied as the dwarf smiled deviously at him. "I prefer the stiletto ... or the gun, sometimes a little poison ... but maybe we shouldn't talk about that now. Maybe we should focus on what we'll be doing when we get to Los Angeles to find the belly dancer. My uncle has made contact with the Casagrande family. We are meeting with Freddy 'Six Fingers' when we arrive. I believe you and he are acquainted ... no? He will fill us in on the plan. Now excuse me, please, Nano. I need to go to the bathroom again."

The dwarf bared his long teeth at Eduardo as if daring him to climb over him, and when Eduardo tried, Nano grabbed his crotch and squeezed till Eduardo sat down again in agony.

Eduardo gulped and said nothing till they landed at LAX and were standing at the luggage carousel. Realizing Nano's arms, long as they were in proportion to his body, weren't quite long enough to reach his bag on the carousel, he said, "here, please, allow me to get that for you."

The dwarf, who was clearly still drunk, curled his lips. He leaped onto the carousel, grabbed the biggest bag Eduardo had ever seen, and hurled it at Eduardo, who staggered back into the luggage cart, causing it to careen off into a crowd of passengers who were waiting for their own bags. Before Eduardo could recover enough to apologize, Nano had sprung over to where the cart had pinned an old woman to the wall. She screamed at him and tried to hit him with her walking stick, which he grabbed and snapped in two as if it were a toothpick. After he snarled at her, she kept very quiet.

*Sweet mother of Jesus,* thought Eduardo, *the dwarf will get us arrested before we even find the belly dancer. What the hell was my uncle thinking?* He made a note to call the marchese and ask him how he was supposed to work with Nano.

Nano's bag weighed a ton and Eduardo, despite his strength, struggled to get it on the cart alongside his carryon. He wondered what it was the dwarf had packed, but the bomb-sniffing dog checking out bags paid no attention to Nano's bag, instead electing to walk up behind him and sniff his ass. uch to the amusement of other passengers, and to the absolute horror of Eduardo, Nano made a grab for the dog, spun it around, and began to sniff its ass, until the dog managed to wriggle free and ran off, yelping and dragging its handler behind it.

They were met in the arrival hall by a tall young man with curly black hair. He was dressed in a white linen suit that made him look more like a French Riviera dilettante than a Los Angeles mobster. He smiled at Eduardo, and looked warily at the dwarf.

"I'm Bobby Casagrande," he said, shaking Eduardo's hand. "I hope you had a good trip."

"Eduardo Sabatini at your service. And this gentleman is Nano Mortale."

"Aha, the famous midget hitman." Bobby held his hand out to Nano, who ignored it completely and bared his teeth.

"I don't believe he likes to be called a midget...," Eduardo whispered to Bobby. "Hitman is probably sufficient."

"Everyone is so sensitive these days. I'm telling you, Eduardo, Los Angeles is the capital of sensitivity. But I would have thought you Europeans were a little more open. My apologies, Nano. I swear I won't call you a midget again ... ow, fuck!

Nano had sunk his sizeable teeth into Bobby's leg and blood was staining the pure white linen. The bite, though painful, was quick.

"My God, he's insane. I may need a rabies shot."

"That is entirely possible, although I am not sure that rabies is one of the diseases carried by dwarves. What I can tell you is you will need a new suit. That is where I can help. I have an excellent tailor in Rome."

"Thanks," said Bobby, dabbing at his wound with a handkerchief he'd taken from his top pocket. "I may take you up on that at some point. These pants are ruined. Anyway, my father is expecting you. I'll drive with you to his house where we will have lunch and I'll fill you in on our progress. But if I begin to foam at the mouth, please call a doctor."

They walked out to where a stretch limo had pulled up at the curb. A driver in a smart black uniform got out and opened the trunk and back door. Nano didn't even bother to help load his bag, getting into the car and promptly falling fast asleep on the seat. The good news for both Bobby and Eduardo was that he didn't take up much space. The bad news was that he snored incredibly loudly.

# CHAPTER 8

Los Angeles around the same time.
*When looking for answers, it's best not to drink and derive.*

While waiting anxiously in the United lounge at JFK, Charley's rational mind returned just briefly enough for him to make a reservation at the Sunset Hermitage, a small boutique hotel off Sunset Boulevard in West Hollywood. It was intimate and secluded, ideal for someone looking to stay off the radar. He'd been there a number of times in the past and liked everything about it–except the night manager, Stefan Wanke, who for reasons unknown harbored a deep resentment for Charley. Much to his relief, Wanke was not on duty when he checked in.

"We have a lovely room for you, Mr. Banks," said the young woman at the front desk, whose nametag read 'Jennifer.'

"I hope it's quiet and not overlooking the pool this time?" In Charley's experience, the rooms overlooking the pool were the noisiest in the entire hotel, mostly due to the rock stars and their entourages who frequented the hotel, and were known to launch projectiles from their balconies into the pool as the night's festivities went on. During his last stay, he'd nearly been decapitated by a TV monitor as he sat quietly in one of the chaise lounges enjoying a nightcap.

"No, you specified you wanted something a bit more discreet, so it's right at the back overlooking the garden. How long will you be staying with us this time?"

"I'm not sure. It depends ... let's say three nights, but I may need more."

"Hmm," she said, looking at the computer screen in front of her. "That shouldn't be a problem as long as you give us a day's notice."

"Thanks for being so accommodating, Jennifer. I really appreciate it. Quite a change from when I normally check in. That Wanke guy is awfully aggressive, and I've no idea why. It's rather disconcerting, I have to tell you. I nearly booked somewhere else."

"Stefan, our manager? It's pronounced Vanke by the way. Not Wanker. He gets very upset when people call him Wanker. I have no idea why. Wanker sounds a lot better than Vanke if you ask me. Let's see, yes, he'll be here tonight if you need to talk to him."

"No, I don't really want to talk to him at all if I can help it. But thanks for correcting my pronunciation. That may explain his hostile attitude."

The young lady shrugged indifferently and handed him his key. She offered the services of the bellman to carry Charley's small bag, which Charley declined, believing he'd need to get to know the exact path to the room by himself. Blindfolded, if necessary, he thought. Though he wasn't sure why.

The room as promised was quite isolated, and exactly what Charley had had in mind when he'd constructed his 'Fanny in the Hotel' fantasy during the six-hour flight. He unpacked his clothes and lay down on the bed. It was a large and extremely soft queen covered in a particularly plush green silk spread. He thrust his hips up and down a few times, and concluded it was both springier and cozier than the king-size bed he and Alexandra had shared in New York. It would be a tight squeeze with someone of Fanny's proportions, but a tight squeeze was far preferable to empty space. Having concluded that the bedroom and its accoutrement would actually enhance the 'Fanny in the Bedroom' fantasy, he bounced up and walked into the bathroom. There was a large Jacuzzi that looked inviting, and it would have had fantasy potential had he not examined the cavernous steam shower with its four individual pulsating heads positioned at tit and ass level. Charley took out one of the *Porky Asses* pages that featured Fanny posing provocatively in a bathroom full of pink chintz. He held it up against the shower stall. The décor was possibly a little mimimalist for Fanny, but there was absolutely no doubt in Charley's mind that she would be ecstatic at the Sunset Hermitage.

The now familiar stirring of his libido every time he looked at Fanny, on which he'd kept a tight rein since the night before, erupted like a roman candle. When he was done and in a less distracted frame of mind, he took out the card on which he'd written the number for Nolan Publications. He took a deep breath and dialed.

The phone rang for a long time before someone picked up and the line almost immediately disconnected. Charley checked the number and dialed again. The exact same thing happened. The third time he managed to yell out before the call was cut off.

"Please don't hang up. I'm trying to get ahold of Nolan Publications."

"Si," said the voice on the other end.

"Is this Nolan Publications?"

"Si."

"Sorry, my Spanish isn't great, but I'd like to come in and speak with the publisher."

"Si."

"Great, when would be convenient?"

"Que?"

"Okay?" Charley was getting confused. "But when?"

"Si."

"I don't understand. I need to see the editor of one of your magazines ... is there someone there who speaks English?" The line went dead again. Charley tried calling back a few times, but no one answered. The only alternative to another frustrating hang-up was to go in person and take his chances that someone would see him without an appointment. He called the front desk, asked them to get him a taxi, and within fifteen minutes was on his way to the address he'd so carefully written down. The sun was setting over Hollywood, but in Charley's mind it was commencement of what he hoped would be the most exciting chapter of his life.

Nolan publications was in a run-down building, sandwiched between a Thai restaurant and an electronic store, on Santa Monica, just south of La Brea. The sign on the door indicated that the studio was on the first floor and reception on the second. He wondered if Fanny was in the studio and trying out different poses. Just before his imagination got the better of him, he reined it in and climbed the rickety staircase to the second floor, where the sign on the glass door read *Nolan Pub. Inc. Publishers of Refined and Not-soRefined Literature.* The door was locked, though there were lights on in the back. He could just make out what looked like a comfortable reception area with two white couches and an empty desk with an old-fashioned typewriter. He knocked loudly but no one appeared. There was a hum coming from somewhere in the office, which he thought sounded like a vacuum cleaner. It stopped, and after a minute or two a woman in a cleaner's uniform appeared through a doorway behind the reception desk. He knocked again and waved at her until she shuffled over to the door and unlocked it.

"Si?" It was the same voice he'd heard when he called.

"Look, I spoke to you earlier. I'm trying to get ahold of someone at Nolan Publications...?" Charley spoke slowly and deliberately, hoping to make his question clearer. He desperately tried to think of the appropriate words and cursed the fact that he'd never really done more with his high school Spanish.

"She open a las diez," the old woman said, pointing at the ten on her watch.

"Ten o'clock tomorrow morning?"

"No, diez de esta noche."

"Aha." He finally understood. Of course, a sex magazine would operate in the dark hours. "So if I come back...." But the woman had shut the door and locked it.

Charley looked at his own watch and groaned. It was only 6:20. What the hell was he going to do for the nearly four hours? The thought of going back to the hotel alone was too depressing. Then he remembered the little Thai restaurant next door and decided he'd hang out there. He was pretty famished in any case.

The food was remarkably good and for a long time he was the only customer. He ordered leisurely and tried his best to sip the martinis as slowly as he could. But four hours is a long time to pace yourself, and by the time he finally looked at his watch and saw it was five after ten, he was pretty much hammered.

# CHAPTER 9

Los Angeles, same time.
*The dangers that lie in lies themselves.*

This time the lights were on and there was a woman behind the reception desk. She looked up through her thick black-rimmed glasses as Charley knocked politely and stuck his head round the door.

"Can I help you?" Her voice was guarded, though not unfriendly

For a moment Charley was convinced he was at the wrong place. The woman looked to be in her early forties with dull-brown hair drawn up tightly in a ponytail. Her dress was dark blue with a white collar. More suited to the organizer of the Women's' Temperance Society at the local church than the receptionist at a publisher of pornographic magazines, he thought.

"Yes, you can, or at least I hope you can." Charley tried not to slur his words. "I want to speak to the publisher about a writing job. I'm a writer, you see."

"Have you been drinking?"

"Umm, no, not really. Just a glass of wine while I was waiting at the Thai restaurant. Maybe two. It's more jet lag. I flew in from New York this afternoon."

"Oh, well that's good, because Mrs. Nolan won't see you if you're drunk. She doesn't approve of strong liquor."

"Definitely not drunk. Quite sober, I assure you. Not big on liquor my shelf, I mean myself." Charley was once again speaking very slowly, trying to enunciate each word, but not doing particularly well.

"May I make a suggestion then?"

"Of course, go right ahead, but rest assured it's just jet lag."

She smiled sympathetically. "You say you're a writer?"

"I am. I am a writer. Written for some pretty famous publications. Like *Prayboy* and...."

"Did you say Pray Boy?"

"I don't think so...." His tongue felt thick and he knew the words weren't coming out right.

"Good, because we don't publish magazines of a homosexual nature in this office. That's Mr. Nolan's brother's business in Kansas. Although I think the gay religious magazine he publishes is called *Ah Men*."

"I meant to say *Playboy*. It's not a gay magazine."

"The point is, our magazines don't really have a lot of writing. Just some headlines here and there. They're photographic essays, as Mrs. Nolan calls them. So I'm going to make a suggestion." She beckoned him conspiratorially. "I'll tell Mrs. Nolan that you're here to try out as a model. She's going to like you a lot. You're different from most of the other men who come in. More ... normal-looking. But don't tell her I told you. Promise?"

"Of course." Charley's head was swimming in a primordial soup of vodka and confusion. "I won't say a word. But I can't be a model."

"Oh yes, you can. You're clean and you're quite good-looking. Very different to the garbage that normally comes in. You just need to brush your hair. Here...."

She took a large hairbrush from her handbag and handed it to Charley, who made an attempt to brush his thick hair, which was overdue for a cut.

"Now do the back as well. Yes, that's much better. Oh, she's going to love you."

Charley blushed. Try as he might, he couldn't quite see himself as a model for a skin magazine, and yet there appeared to be no alternative at this moment if he was going to talk to Mrs. Nolan. He attempted a smile, but before he'd even had time to mumble an agreement, she'd pushed a button on the phone.

"Mrs. Nolan, there's a model here to see you. Oh, yes. I think you're going to like him for the part. Fine, I'll send him back."

She put the phone down and gave Charley a wink. "Straight through this door and down the hall. You'll see a bright pink door. Just knock and walk in. You're expected."

As drunk as he was, Charley realized that he had no real game plan whatsoever for the speed at which things were moving. But it was too late to turn back now. He was at the bright pink door and it was open

"Don't just stand there gaping. Close your mouth and come in."

If the receptionist had unnerved him, Mrs. Nolan sucked the air clean out his lungs.

She was the doppelgänger of his great-grandmother, or as he remembered her from a photo on the mantle above the fireplace at his mother's house in Connecticut. Her close-cropped hair was white and her glasses looked like they'd been cut from the bottoms of Coca Cola bottles. A pale puce-colored dress completed the picture, and like that of the receptionist, was tightly buttoned at the neck, as if the mere hint of flesh was abhorrent. She stood up slowly from behind a desk strewn with photographs that Charley couldn't quite make out from where he stood, frozen to the spot.

"Come in, sweetheart, don't be shy. Ooh, yes. You'll be wonderful. You're a nice big boy with lots of space to work on. Portia is going to love you." Her voice was thick like old buttermilk, with a distinct Southern twang.

"Umm, I'm not sure what you mean by work on? Is Portia a makeup artist?"

She cackled. "Oh, that's a ripe one. Portia? A makeup artist? You're funny. Now, you don't have AIDS, do you?"

"What?"

"I said, do you have AIDS?"

"Do I have AIDS...?"

"Listen, young man. I'm eighty-five years old and I can hear better than a Catholic priest at a whore's confession. Don't tell me you're deaf and got AIDS."

"I'm not deaf," said Charley, recovering slightly. "No one's ever asked me that before."

"Crap, everyone asks those questions these days. Where've you worked recently?"

"Umm, mainly at home but also in Africa and Europe."

"Well then, you're sure to have AIDS. That's not going to work with Portia."

"Look, Mrs. Nolan, I guarantee you I don't have AIDS. No venereal diseases at all...." His voice faded as he suddenly caught sight of some of the objects strewn around the office.

A collection of rubber penises and dildos, ranging from a small green one the length of an index finger to a monstrous mule-sized purple one shimmering with sequins, were displayed like museum pieces on a wooden bookshelf. Various leather outfits hung like discarded skin from a clothing rack against the wall, and a bin filled with studded hot pants and evil-looking whips and riding crops was pushed into a corner.

"Hey." She snapped her bony fingers. "I said, hey. I'm talking to you, boy. What in damnation is wrong with you?"

"No, no, nothing. I'm just a little jet-lagged. I just got in from New York."

"Well, I suppose that explains why you sound drunk. What's your name?

"It's Charley Brooks, but...."

"Charley Brooks-Butt? Never heard of you. But that's the perfect name for our next publication. Now take your pants down."

'Huh?"

"Damnation, I said take you pants down before I lose my temper. I don't have time for messing around. We're shooting tomorrow."

Her voice carried such authority that without even thinking about it, Charley unbuckled his belt and slowly lowered his pants. Before he could straighten up, Mrs. Nolan, with an agility not normally associated with octogenarians, whirled from behind her desk and pulled down his boxers. She grabbed hold of his penis and examined it closely through her thick glasses. "It doesn't look infected, but it's awfully red. You been working it hard?"

"You could say that."

"Well good, 'cause Portia won't tolerate slackers."

Charley wasn't sure whether slackers in this context referred to lazy people or to soft penises, but he decided not to ask. She'd let go of his penis and he thought it safe to pull up his pants.

"You sure you haven't worked with Portia before?"

"No, I don't think so."

"Oh, believe me, boy, you'd remember. You'd still be smarting and hollering every time you took a poop. Portia, Princess of Pain, is what we call her and you'll be her slave in this...." She held up a galley proof that caused Charley to almost lose his Thai dinner. The cover photo was of a powerful-looking Amazon with pale skin and black hair, dressed in a skimpy leather bikini holding a whip in one hand and a dildo to rival the sequined monster on the shelf in the other. The title read *Portia, Princess of Pain and the Dildo of Doom*. But it wasn't the title that caused Charley's knees to buckle, it was the copy underneath it. *See her whip her slave into a whimpering cur and then rip him a new asshole.*

'What's wrong, boy? You look like you're about to faint? You worried about medical?"

All Charley could manage was a groan.

"Don't worry, we'll have a registered nurse on hand to sew you up good. Now, we pay a hundred an hour for the work and twenty an hour for recovery time. Any questions?"

Through the horror of what he was hearing, Charley knew he needed to be resolute in his mission. "Umm, Mrs. Nolan, that sound's acceptable, but I was kind of hoping I could work with Fanny?"

"Fanny? Who the hell is Fanny?"

Charley's heart stopped yet again. Had Klinkhammer made a mistake? "Fanny Packer? She was in your magazine called *Porky Asses*?"

"Oh, yes that one. No, that's one of Junior's magazines. I just deal with *Bondage and Leather*."

Charley breathed a sigh of relief. At least he was in the right place. "Do you think you could ask Junior? I'm really very keen to see Fanny."

"Hmm, you know something? You're the second person to come in here over the past day or so to ask about her. The other guy was a real greaseball. Something's not right, I can smell it. You wait here, I'll get Junior."

Charley's heart, which had been subject to a large variety of movements over the past two days, sank yet again. Could there possibly be someone else who lusted after Fanny? Surely not. It certainly wasn't a scenario he'd even considered, and wasn't one that he welcomed. Before he had time to contemplate what he was going to do, he heard the door click shut and what sounded like a key turning in the lock.

He whirled around only to find that Mrs. Nolan was no longer in the office, and the pink door was locked. While a survey of possible escape routes should have been his priority right then, his eyes were drawn to the photographs on Mrs. Nolan's desk. He looked closely and gasped as scenes from his worst nightmares played out before him. There were men trussed up like Thanksgiving turkeys, bent over like pretzels, hanging from the ceiling and tied to benches that resembled medieval torture devices. And above them or below them, depending on their positions, stood a leather-clad Portia, Princess of Pain. She smiled in sadistic pleasure as she applied the various instruments of her trade to whatever expanse of flesh happened to be within whip or dildo distance. The men on the other hand, Charley noticed, displayed no signs of outward pleasure. As he moved from one petrifying picture to the next, he felt his balls slowly ascend into his pelvis. None of the photographs shocked him as much though as the one in a silver frame in the middle of the desk. It showed a group of kids frolicking happily on the beach. Across it, in a child's handwriting, was scribbled 'We love you Grammy and Grandpa Nolan.' Charley gagged in abject horror. Did the Nolans' depravity know no bounds? Before he could ponder this important question further, the door burst open and a little old man rushed in. The spittle hanging from his wrinkled mouth terrified Charley less than the sawed-off shotgun he held in his frail hands. Mrs. Nolan was right behind him.

"Why in the name of hell can't you people leave her alone?" Junior, for it could be no one else, pointed the gun as best he could in the general direction of a quaking Charley.

"Don't shoot, please, don't shoot," was all Charley could manage.

"Why shouldn't I? You were going to do a lot worse to her."

"Who, who...."

"You sound like a goddam owl, boy. But you'll be squealing like a pig in a minute."

"I don't want to hurt Fanny, I swear it. I just wanted to talk to her...."

"Talk? Do you take me for a fool? You want to hang her from a meat hook and disembowel her."

"No, no. I just want to...."

"What? Pour gasoline on her and broil her?"

"Blow his balls off, Junior." This from Mrs. Nolan.

"You keep out of this, you old bat. I'm in charge here. First I'm gonna pepper his kneecaps and then maybe I'll blow his balls off."

"Please," gasped Charley. "I don't know who the other people are, but I just want to meet her."

"The only person you're going to meet is your maker, you miserable bastard. Now stand back, woman, and put down that damn dildo."

Mrs. Nolan had grabbed the big sequined dildo off the shelf.

"No chance of that, Junior. I'm gonna shove this so far up his ass it'll come out his head."

"Good Lord, Noleen. You've been editing too many of the Portia magazines. Know what, I'm gonna do this clean." He thrust the barrel of the shotgun in Charley's face.

"No," screamed Mrs. Nolan. "That's too quick. Shoot him here." She pushed the gun down till it pointed at Charley's crotch. But Junior wasn't having any of it. He tried to jerk the barrel out of her hands, but she hung on like a leech. This was the opportunity that Charley needed. He rushed the old couple with such force that they both toppled over onto the carpet. There was a terrific explosion as Junior discharged both barrels, and half the ceiling came down on top of them.

The last thing Charley heard as he bolted down the stairs into the dark Hollywood night was Noleen Nolan berating Junior for being "such a weakling and a pussy."

It was midnight by the time he finally walked into the lobby of the Sunset Hermitage feeling as if his life was basically over.

# CHAPTER 10

Beverly Hills, earlier that same day.
*When a helping hand has an extra finger.*

Eduardo had grown somewhat accustomed to the outlandish taste of his American colleagues while working with the Gambino family, but nothing he'd seen had prepared him for the house of Freddy "Six Fingers" Casagrande. It lay in a quiet cul-de-sac behind enormous iron gates that seemed solid enough to stop a tank. Two guards who could have been recruited from the set of *The Godfather* opened the gates and waved cheerily to Bobby as the limo made its way up the yellow-brick driveway amidst a pleasant and extremely lush garden. The carefully laid flowerbeds surrounded what at first appeared to be ill-cut bushes, but on closer inspection turned out to be hedges trimmed to resemble outlandish animals.

"You like my dad's safari park?" Bobby asked, disentangling his left foot from Nano, who'd rolled off the seat onto the floor.

"Well, it's certainly unusual," said Eduardo. He was trying to determine if the closest hedge was a lion

chasing a herd of wildebeest or a deformed dog chasing a pack of long-legged rabbits.

"My father is an unusual man. He loves animals, so
instead of becoming a big game hunter like some of
our colleagues, who fill their houses with heads and
skins, he decided he would create the African Savan-
nah here in Beverley Hills. You must admit he has a
talent for topiary."

"I'm afraid I am not familiar with that word."

"The art of trimming bushes and hedges to resemble animals."

"What skill he must have." Eduardo was trying to
make out a hedge that could have been a hippopota-
mus or a sheep. "I marvel that a man who is missing
four fingers can wield a hedge trimmer with such ar-
tistry."

"Why do you think my father is missing four fingers?"

"He is called Freddy 'Six Fingers,' is he not?

"Yes, but because he has six fingers on his one
hand, not because he is missing any. A lot of people
think the sixth digit is what gives him the ability to
trim bushes so perfectly. But if I were you I would not
look at his hand. He is extremely conscious of his extra finger and doesn't take kindly to people who react
badly. Trust me, don't even glance. It would not be a
good start to your visit."

Bobby reminded Eduardo of Marco "Baby Face"
Modesto, the one member of the Gambino family
he'd actually liked. Both were refined, as much as
mobsters could be refined, and projected a quiet
confidence that contrasted dramatically with the

brash swagger most of the American mobsters see-med to have.

The limo pulled up to a sprawling pink mansion that could have been designed by the architect of Caesar's Palace while high on LSD. At that moment Nano woke up.

"We are at my father's house, Nano."

Nano looked out the window and grunted. Then he began to squeeze his crotch as if he needed to pee.

"You should have gone at the airport, Nano." Eduardo sounded like an embarrassed parent. Some-how, he felt the dwarf was his responsibility.

Nano responded with his usual snarl and, pushing Eduardo and Bobby aside, loped like one of the strange garden animals through the gilded white front door of the house, held open by a uniformed butler.

"Don't worry about the luggage," Bobby said. "Leave it in the car, and after lunch the driver will take you to your hotel. We booked you in to the Sun-set Hermitage. A small hotel, very out the way. Ah, look, here is my father."

The butler had moved aside to reveal a man who was very much an older but tougher version of Bob-by. Freddy "Six Fingers" was tall and imposing, with a shock of long white hair and a big toothy grin. His one hand was in his pocket and in the other he held a lethal-looking set of hedge clippers.

"Eduardo Sabatini, what an honor to have you at my house."

"Don Casagrande, the honor is mine." Eduardo ex-tended his hand, but the smiling don pushed it aside and wrapped him in a bear-hug, causing the point of the hedge clippers to dig sharply into Eduardo's buttocks.

"Come in, my boy, and please forgive the humbleness of my home. It doesn't compare to your palazzo, I am sure."

Eduardo couldn't disagree with Freddy "Six Fingers" on that point. His palazzo had been in his family for five centuries, and its elegance reflected the spoils of ill-gotten loot and the aristocratic tastes of generations of Sabatinis. The Casagrande mansion, on the other hand, looked like the home of someone who'd spent far too much time in a Turkish brothel. It was hard to tell whether the gold-plated fixtures complemented the purple velvet and white leather furniture or insulted it. Eduardo made what he felt was a very polite and restrained gesture as he looked around the vast living room. No taste always bypassed bad taste on the road to absolutely awful taste. He took a deep breath and tried to slow his heartbeat. Once he had calmed down sufficiently, his attention was drawn to a collection of bonsai trees. Finally, he thought, something a little more restrained. He smiled at the don and pointed with an open hand at the little trees, then bent down to take a closer look. They were not, as he had first surmised, sculptured trees, but rather miniature versions of the same bizarre animal sculptures from the garden.

"Ah, I see you like my Bonsai Beasts...." Don Casagrande took what looked like a slightly larger version a nose-hair trimmer out his pocket and begun to snip

tiny leaves off a frog-shaped bonsai. "It is a new hob-
by of mine, but one I feel I am perfectly suited to."

He picked up the tiny sculpture and held it out to
Eduardo.

"Here, look closely and tell me what it is."

"Magnificent, Don Casagrande. You have a real
skill." Eduardo bent forward to examine the frog—or
perhaps locust—and suddenly shrank back in terror.
Creeping around the side of the little pot was something positively nightmarish: the hirsute sixth-finger
that had inspired colleagues of Fredo Pietro Daniele
Casagrande to affectionately bestow upon him his
sobriquet. To Eduardo it was as if he'd come face to
face with the leg of a huge diabolical tarantula. He
gasped in horror and shrunk back.

"What's wrong, Eduardo?" There was a hint of ve-
nom in the don's voice, and Eduardo immediately remembered Bobby's warning about not reacting to the
digitally enhanced don.

"Oh, Madonna. Nothing is wrong, Don Casagrande." Eduardo swallowed and recovered his com-
posure. "I am just so surprised at how wonderfully
realistic this ... frog is. It almost scared me for a moment ... hah."

"Okay, okay, it's actually a penguin ... but it is realistic, no?"

"Incredible. You are a master of the clipper. Tell
me, please, where did you learn your art?"

Bobby, who'd been smiling through the whole epi-
sode, laughed. "My dad first started using a clipper
when dealing with some members of a Colombian
cartel who thought they might like to do business

in Los Angeles. You could say they ended up being members of the cartel without their members."

Eduardo shuddered, but Don Casagrande laughed and pinched his son's cheek. "Bobby, you'd be a funny boy if you weren't such a sensitive, touchy sap. Now come, let's have lunch by the pool and we can tell you what we know about your belly dancer. Where is that damn Nano? Last I saw him he was trying to piss in the geraniums."

As the don turned away, Eduardo noticed Bobby's face had turned grey and his eyes were screwed up as if he was in pain. He patted Bobby on the shoulder and smiled at him with the sympathy that only someone who truly knows abuse can have. Bobby understood and smiled back.

Nano Mortale was lying on a chaise by the pool, with a half empty bottle of vodka in his hand. He'd taken off his shirt, and for the first time Eduardo was able to identify what made him so strong. His chest, shoulders and arms, though covered in thick reddish hair, showed a network of enormous muscles. His body was not so much like that of a bodybuilder as it was like the orangutan Eduardo had seen at the zoo in Rome when his uncle had taken him there as a child. He quickly looked away when the dwarf noticed him staring.

"Come, Nano. Come sit with us and eat. You can't survive on liquor." Don Casagrande pointed to the table that was spread with plates of antipasti and bottles of Lambrusco. "Sit, Eduardo, and we can eat and talk."

The dwarf did not acknowledge the invitation as the other three sat down. A maid in a starched uniform passed plates around while the don poured the sparkling red wine. Only a minute later did Nano toss the empty bottle into the pool and come over to the table. He snatched the plate of antipasto and began to shovel it into his mouth with his hands. Then he grabbed one of the bottles of Lambrusco and poured most of it into his water tumbler. Eduardo glanced at Don Casagrande, but the don either didn't care or was pretending not to notice.

"How is your uncle, Eduardo? I haven't seen him for ages."

Eduardo was having a hard time concentrating on what the don was saying as he watched Nano attack the food and wine.

"Um, my uncle...?"

"Yes, yes. Your uncle, the marchese?"

"Ah, yes, that uncle." Eduardo forced his mind back to the moment.

"Of course, that uncle. How many uncles do you have?"

"Well, just the one ... and that one, he is very well, thank you. Very busy."

"I can see you are jet-lagged, Eduardo. Let's finish eating. We can fill you in on our progress and then you can go take a nap."

After the empty plates of antipasti had been cleared, the maid came out with a large bowl of spaghetti alla vongole. Before she could serve, Nano grabbed a handful of clams, put them in his mouth, and then spat them out in disgust. He picked up the half-full bottle of Lambrusco and went back to his chaise by the pool.

"Not everyone likes shellfish, I guess," said Bobby, his disdain for Nano evident.

"Yes, I should have thought about that," said the don. "He prefers snails to shellfish. I just remembered shells."

"We should probably get him to come back if you're going to fill us in on what you've found out, don't you think?" asked Eduardo.

"No, no, leave him. Nano is a hands-on guy. He doesn't really contribute much to the planning." They all looked over towards Nano, who had fallen asleep with his hand down the front of his pants. Don Casagrande shrugged and poured what was left of the Lambrusco into his glass. "Bobby, why don't you tell our friend where we are with the belly dancer."

"Sure, Dad. I wish I could say we have her in the basement here, but we don't." He noticed Eduardo's disappointment. "It's not all bad. Don't worry, Eduardo. We're close. What we know is that she is still here in Los Angeles and she recently went to see a publishing company that she'd worked for in the past. Unfortunately, the man we sent to interview the owners suffered a severe shotgun blast to his knees, but not before being told that she was working somewhere in Los Angeles."

"A publishing company? You don't think she could be trying to sell the book?"

"It's not that kind of publishing company," laughed Bobby. "These guys publish magazines with names like *The Bone Ranger*...."

The don laughed. "Bobby, maybe you should buy some of those magazines. They might help you with the ladies. If you ever decided to date one."

Bobby rolled his eyes. "Thanks, Dad. I appreciate your concern."

His father grimaced.

"But it's a big city, how will you find her?" Eduardo asked, trying to alleviate the awkwardness of the moment.

"Sorry, Eduardo. Yes, it is. But she's got to be dancing, and there aren't that many Middle-Eastern restaurants that have belly dancers. We should know more latest tomorrow."

"Okay, well, I appreciate all that you're both doing. Tomorrow is probably better. I'm definitely feeling the jet lag."

"So why don't we try to get your companion and you checked into the hotel. You can rest, and we'll regroup tomorrow morning."

"That's fine by me. Who can tell with Nano Mortale though? He is a difficult man to understand."

"Let me talk to him," said Don Casagrande. "He and I have an understanding."

"That's a relief," Bobby said. "I can't understand a thing he grunts, and he sure as hell doesn't talk English."

"Or Italian," Eduardo laughed.

"It's hard," replied the don. "He understands everything, but it's true he doesn't say much. Look, don't be too tough on him, boys. He's had a hard life, and he's extremely loyal to your uncle." He paused as if thinking back. "He saved my life once."

"You never told me that. What happened?" asked Bobby.

"It's a long story. I'll tell you one of these days. Maybe at your bachelor party." The don laughed, though it wasn't a pleasant laugh.

# CHAPTER 11

Beverley Hills, that night and the next day.
*From disillusionment comes enlightenment.*

Charley arrived back at the Sunset Hermitage still quaking from his close encounter with Junior Nolan's shotgun and his wife's giant dildo. In the taxi, he'd come to the devastating realization that his pursuit of Fanny was at an end. Though he'd sobered up somewhat, his disheveled appearance and hang-dog expression caught the attention of his arch-nemesis, Stefan Wanke.

"Ah, Mr. Brooks. I heard you'd checked in. I would welcome you back, but you do not seem to be very convivial at the moment."

"I'm not in the least bit convivial. I have an awful headache and I just want to go to bed. So if it's all the same to you, Mr. Wanke—or Vanke—I won't engage in small talk."

"That is of course your right, but I shall be watching you."

"Why the hell would you be vatching me?"

"To make sure that your behavior does not interfere with the peace and quiet our other guests' desire. We have a very sophisticated Italian aristocrat who checked in this afternoon with his manservant. I would hate him to get the wrong impression of us through some of the people we are forced to accept."

"Well, screw him and you. I'm going to bed." Charley pushed past the bespectacled little German and made his way to his room. As he opened the door, the reality of his situation hit him again squarely on the chin. Fanny in the bedroom or Fanny in any other part of his life was over. He felt like a complete fool. How the hell could someone who was normally rational and reasonably mature fall into such an emotional bear-trap? He lay back on the bed hoping to pass out quickly, but as soon as he turned on his side he heard the crackle of the *Porky Asses* pages he'd stuffed under the pillow before he'd left. There was no possible way he could look at them again, and so shielding his eyes as best he could, he crumpled them up and tossed them into the waste basket. Then, in what an observer of deviant behavior might have called a ritualistic cleansing ceremony, Charley got off the bed, stripped naked, and set fire to the pages.

A tired mind is a lazy mind, and a lazy mind tends to overlook what is blatantly obvious to someone of a more refreshed disposition: plastic-coated pages and lit matches are a deadly combination. Fanny's bottom began to boil and splutter in a most horrendous way, and the fire alarm directly above the small but impressive conflagration began to wail in protest as flames and thick, acrid smoke filled the room. Charley panicked and picked up the metal waste basket, which by now was almost red hot. He rushed into the bathroom, screaming in pain as the hot metal began to sear his flesh, and threw the waste basket into the bathtub. Before he could turn on the faucet, the cloth shower curtain caught fire. At this point Charley started to pass out from the dioxin, a further byproduct of plastic and flames. Babbling like a madman, he stumbled towards the door, which at that moment burst open as hotel staff with fire extinguishers rushed into the room spraying thick carpets of foam in front of them. Charley managed to jump back and cover his genitals, but his feet slid on the foam and he careened across the floor head first into a large red fire extinguisher operated by Stefan Wanke. Then a warm, comforting darkness overtook him.

Sunlight forced its way through his heavy eyelids. "Alexandra, please don't open the blinds ... I just want to sleep."

"He's coming round." The voice, unlike Alexandra's Long Island whine, had a distinctly German accent. Charley opened his eyes to see the scowling face of Stefan Wanke. As his vision focused, he realized that the light was coming from a pencil-flashlight held by an older man sitting on the edge of the bed.

"What's going on? What happened?"

"Relax, pal," said the older man. "You hit your head pretty badly on the fire extinguisher. Remember?"

"Oh, Jesus, yes." Suddenly everything about the night before came back to Charley and his stomach heaved. He put his hand up to his head and felt a lump the size of an egg.

"Good. Well, you don't appear to have a concussion, and you're lucky you hit a rounded object or you'd have split your skull. I can't feel any fracture, but I'm a dermatologist not a surgeon. So go and get yourself checked out at a hospital and try to stay in bed and rest until lunchtime. Mr. Wanke, maybe you should get him some tea."

"Of course, Doctor. I will ring for some and then you and I, Mr. Brooks, we need to have a serious chat about damages."

"For Christ's sake, man," said the doctor, standing up. "I don't think he's in any shape to have a serious chat. And as for damages, you'll be lucky if he doesn't sue you for assault with a fire extinguisher."

That last statement by the doctor caused Wanke to pause. "Umm, no, of course it was all an accident. We will not be suing Mr. Brooks for damages nor will he, I'm sure, be suing us. I just want to make sure we are all on the same page. And Doctor, I would like to offer you and your wife dinner at our fine restaurant for your trouble."

"No trouble," replied the doctor. "But I will take you up on the dinner. Especially with how much you're charging for the room. It's quite outrageous. Anyway," this to Charley, "take it easy and try to sleep. You'll feel better when you wake up."

Wanke showed the doctor to the door and returned to Charley's bedside. "We will call things even, Mr. Brooks, but the hotel is full from tomorrow, so you will check out in the morning. I will have your clothes brought here from the damaged room." And with that he walked out, slamming the door behind him.

Charley wasn't particularly phased by Wanke's pronouncement of eviction. There was absolutely no reason to stay in Los Angeles any longer. He yawned, closed his eyes, and fell into a deep and untroubled sleep.

When he finally awoke and looked at his watch, he saw it was nearly 6:30. He'd slept for almost ten hours. Other than needing to pee badly, he felt surprisingly calm and refreshed. Almost as if the fire had cleansed him of his bedeviling obsession with Fanny. Though his head still hurt a little and the bump, if anything, felt slightly larger than it had that morning, all in all he was back to his normal self. He even thought of calling Alexandra and trying to make up, but decided he'd probably burnt that bridge for good. Surprisingly, that didn't bother him either. This was an opportunity to truly start over. Find new friends, new lovers. But first, find a place to eat. He was starving.

Thirty minutes later, freshly showered and dressed in a comfortable pair of jeans, sneakers and a worn, though expensive, navy cashmere sweater, he ambled out of the hotel, up the hill and onto Sunset Boulevard. It was a warm, clear evening and he decided to walk towards Beverly Hills, in exactly the opposite direction of Nolan Publications. He had no desire to relive the horror that had bored into his brain like a tapeworm, consuming his powers of reasoning.

Yes, Charley Brooks was back, and most importantly he was free. Perhaps he wouldn't even go back to New York. He could write from anywhere he chose and simply send his stories to anyone who wanted them. Maybe it was time to cover a war once again. God knew there were plenty of those going on. Option followed option and pretty soon his head was swimming in them. But options, as the old Zen saying goes, lead to insanity. And so he stopped thinking and simply looked for a restaurant.

At that very moment a sweet and pungent, though not unpleasant, odor assailed his senses. He looked around to see where it was coming from and realized he'd stopped in front of a restaurant with the words *Mi Casablanca e su Casablanca. Fine Mexican Moroccan Food* painted on the frosted window. He tried to stare through the window, but couldn't make out anything inside. He hesitated for but a moment before the tantalizing and strangely exotic smells forced him to open the door.

"Table for one?" The voice came from a short man with a huge black handlebar mustache and a tatty fez on his head.

"Um, yes." Charley hesitated. "Maybe I could take a quick look at the menu before I sit down...?"

"Not possible," replied the small man. "No menu."

"Well, maybe I'll just come back...."

"No." The man grabbed Charley's elbow and steered him into the rather gloomy interior where, much to Charley's dismay, there were no chairs, just cushions scattered around low tables.

"Don't worry, you like the food. My wife, she is Mexican, and I am from Morocco. The food, it is a mixture of both. It is out of this world, my friend. You sit here." He indicated a large cushion that looked as if it had once been a Persian carpet. "I bring a meal that will take you to places you can't even imagine. You like red wine, yes?"

"Oh, um yes. That will be fine." As dubious as he was about the entire idea of Mexican-Moroccan food and the potential health issues posed by the dust and grime on the floor, Charley felt strangely attracted to the place, and so he plonked down on the cushion and looked around at the other diners.

There were only eight low tables he could see through the low light that emanated from an array of colorful souk-style hanging lanterns. Only three had guests lounging around them. One was occupied by an older Middle-Eastern couple who were picking at a large platter of something that could easily have been a sheep's head surrounded by nachos. There was a much younger group of Hispanic men at another, drinking bottles of Sol beer and laughing loudly. The remaining table was to Charley's left, next to what looked like a small stage. Two men, one in a dark suit and the other in a tank top that showed his bulging muscles to their full effect, were whispering to each other. They stopped when they noticed Charley staring at them. He turned away quickly.

At that moment, the owner appeared with a bottle of wine and the first course. "Here," he said, pulling the cork from the bottle. "It is a fine Moroccan Carignan. You will like. And this is hummus spiced with

habanero and served with corn tortillas. Very good."
He hovered, waiting for Charley to taste.

Charley scooped up a large dollop of the hummus
with a tortilla and almost fainted. The hummus was
so intensely hot that he felt as if the wax in his ears
was melting. He took a swig of the wine to cool his
mouth and tried to say something to the proprietor
through his tears, but he couldn't form words

"Ah, you like it, hey? Take smaller bite, my suggestion. Next course, very flavorful but very mild. And
very soon, the belly dancer comes out. You will love
her. They say she can tell ten stories with her titties
alone, and fifteen when she includes her buttocks. I
go to speed her up." With that he left Charley alone
to work his way through the pain.

Once he'd got the measure of the atomic hummus,
Charley found himself enjoying it immensely. The
heat from the habaneros was intense but in the right
proportion, wrapped in the soft tortilla and tempered by the fruitiness of the Carignan. The second
course arrived, a mole chicken served on a bed of
couscous. After three bites, Charley decided he was
absolutely blown away by the incredible blending of
tastes and wondered if he could do a story on the
restaurant. At least the trip wouldn't be a total waste.

Suddenly his musing was cut short as the lanterns
dimmed and the stage erupted in light and music. A
large shape moved from behind an elaborate screen,
swaying to the rhythmic beat of cymbals and drums
coming from two tinny speakers. The belly dancer's
arrival brought a swift silence to the diners as she
shimmied across the stage, her formidable body ba-

rely hidden by the diaphanous, green and purple silk skirt held up around her waist by a belt strung with coins that clinked in sync to the music. If it were possible to make her look any more exquisite, the tasseled top that displayed her décolletage with every undulating movement did the trick. He was mesmerized by the sinuous rolling of her stomach and percussive shifting of her hips, and while he could not see her entire face behind the veil, the shape of her eyes seemed familiar. He leaned forward. As she turned around, and his focus was drawn to her swaying bottom, he knew exactly who she was.

"Ladies and gentlemen," said an unseen voice that sounded like the proprietor. "Mi Casablanca presents the one and only, the magnificent Miss Fanny Packer!"

The tingling started in Charley's chest, and within seconds had moved down to his crotch. His heart thumped against his ribcage and his breathing slowed as if he were in a dream. This was it. This was her. His search was over

Unfortunately for Charley, it was also over for the two thugs at the next table. As if in a perfectly timed and synchronized movement, Charley and the two men from the table closest to the stage stood up, gasped, and rushed the stage simultaneously.

# CHAPTER 12

Los Angeles, later that same day.
*Flights of fantasy are nonrefundable.*

Charley didn't realize precisely what was happening and for a precious few seconds he was blind to everything but reaching Fanny.

"Fanny, please wait," he pleaded as he put his hand out. She paused for less than a second, took one look at what was happening, shrieked, and fled back behind the screen. Charley rushed after her, followed closely by the two men who had now drawn their guns.

By this point Fanny had made it into the kitchen. Still howling in panic, she crashed into the little Moroccan owner, who spilled a large bowl of steaming couscous onto his wife. She howled in pain and fell onto the floor. Charley, mad with lust and confusion, hurdled over the chef just as the other two men crashed through the kitchen door. The first one slipped on the couscous and slid head first across the floor into the refrigerator. The second one fired a shot and then stopped to help his friend who was lying on the floor bleeding from a large gash in his head. At that moment, the chef stabbed him in the thigh with a kitchen knife.

Charley missed all of this, as by now he was through the back door and into the alley, desperately yelling for Fanny, who was a hundred yards ahead of him, to stop. She was remarkably agile for her size, and it seemed she'd easily evade Charley until she crashed into a garbage can and toppled over.

Charley, panting heavily, stumbled up to where she lay. She covered her face in fear, despite his soft murmurs for her not to be scared. At that moment, the back door to the restaurant opened and the two men staggered out. One was wobbling and clutching his bloody head and the other dragging his leg, but both were still armed and fired at Charley and Fanny. Charley felt a sharp pain in his arm and lurched into the alley wall. He howled in agony and Fanny, who still hadn't moved, suddenly jumped up and grabbed his hand.

"Come on," she said. "We have to move."

Whether Fanny could sense that he meant her no harm, or if she simply felt that any potential ally was better than nothing under the current circumstances, was unclear to Charley. But to his surprise, and as much delight as he could muster with the threat of another bullet coming his way, she clutched his hand tightly and pulled him out the alley and onto Sunset. There was no talk between them as they pushed their way past the trendy crowds who were lining up outside the bars and comedy clubs. A few people stared at Fanny, whose elaborate costume did little to hide her ample curves, but most expected to see weirdly dressed individuals on Sunset, and so didn't give them a second glance.

Charley looked back to see if the two men were following them, but he could see no trace. He felt something warm trickling down his arm, and to his horror realized it was blood. He stopped, and Fanny turned to look at him.

"Ooh, you're bleeding. Let me look."

"I think I've been shot."

Fanny pulled Charley over into the doorway of a building and examined his arm. The navy cashmere sweater was ripped about halfway up his right bicep and blood was trickling out. In a movement that nearly dislocated his shoulder, Fanny tore off the sleeve, exposing a nasty gash.

"Ow, Christ," yelled Charley.

"Oh, come on," replied Fanny, dabbing at the gash with her veil. "Here, let me tie this round your arm. It's just a scratch. It doesn't hurt that much."

"That's easy for you to say. It's really sore. But we have to get out of here, those guys can't be far behind us. Let's go."

"No," said Fanny. "I'm not going anywhere."

"What do you mean? We're in danger ... we have to go."

"No, we don't. For a start, I don't even know you."

"Yes, you do." As he said it, Charley realized he'd made an awful slip. He knew Fanny, but how in the hell could she know him?

"No, I don't.... What's going on? Something isn't right."

Charley had rehearsed his answer on the plane and in the hotel, but not while being chased by dangerous lunatics with Fanny's veil tied round his arm to staunch a bleeding gunshot wound. He tried to think of something and decided on at least some of the truth. "My name's Charley Brooks, I'm a writer and please trust me ... I swear I'm not going to hurt you."

Fanny looked him in the eye as if she were a lawyer cross-examining a witness. "Hmm, I don't know. You seem nice but...." She was interrupted by a yell from down the block as the two wounded goons staggered onto Sunset and caught sight of their quarry. "Oh, good Lord, let's go."

"This way," cried Charley, "my hotel's this way."

He took her arm and the two of them began to run back down Sunset towards the Sunset Hermitage. Running may not have been the most apt description of the action that took place. To start, Charley, despite the wound in his arm being more of a graze than a serious laceration, was still lightheaded from the previous night's pandemonium, and Fanny had on Persian slippers with curly toes that were designed more for swaying than running. As handicapped as they were, the Casagrande soldiers were at an even bigger disadvantage. Both had lost major quantities of blood, and though spurred on by the thought of the don's hedge trimmer, their wretched state eventually got the better of them and both collapsed onto the sidewalk.

"Mr. Brooks, this is too much." It was Stefan Wanke who rushed up to Charley and Fanny as they entered the hotel. "You cannot do this in my establishment. Who is this woman and why is she dressed like a ... like a ... circus tent?" He put out his arm to stop them, but Fanny tossed him aside as if he were an old coat.

"Fuck off, Wanke," croaked Charley as they made their way out the back door towards Charley's room. Only two people saw them. One was a waiter retrieving a room service tray that contained an empty vodka bottle, and the other was a half-drunk dwarf who was looking out his second-story window at the garden below. By the time Charley and Fanny had made it to Charley's room, Charley could do nothing but collapse on the bed.

"What a beautiful room. I love it," Fanny said, looking around.

"I knew you would," Charley blurted out before he even knew what he was saying. Since hitting the bed, his mind, previously awash in sheer panic, was now awash in total euphoria.

"You knew I would...? How did you know I would?" Fanny sat down next to him on the bed. "I don't know exactly what's going on here. First you think I should know you and now you say you knew I'd love the room. What aren't you telling me, Charley Brooks?"

Charley looked up into her face and the emotional magma he'd felt when he first picked up *Porky Asses* began to flow through his body once more, deadening the pain in his arm and dulling his brain. If anything, Fanny was more stunning than he could have imagined. She glowed with an almost ethereal beauty. A softness and warmth that he'd never seen in any other woman. Her thick red hair framed the face of a Rubenesque goddess and her body was, he decided, the Three Graces joined as one.

"Look, Fanny, I know this may sound odd and I won't blame you if you decide to walk out the door, though I'm worried those other guys, whoever they are, will find us. But the minute I saw you, something inside me snapped. I can't explain it, honestly. It just did. That's why I felt we must have met." It was not the whole truth but it seemed to do the trick.

She looked at him with a slightly quizzical expression, and took a deep breath.

"Well, it does sound odd, and I'm not sure I believe you entirely. You did try to stop those men, and I suppose you saved my life, but I am going to go. I have a feeling I know who they are and why they're after me. Neither of us will be safe, so you need to go back to wherever you're from and I have to call my friend. I'm really sorry, Charley, but I think it's for the best."

She reached over, picked up the phone, and dialed a number. Charley just stared at her as a great sadness enveloped him. He couldn't bear the thought of losing her, but he had no words to make her stay.

"Hi Paula, it's me, Fanny. Not great, thank you. Sorry to ask, but can you come and get me? I'm not too far ... a hotel called, uh...." She read the name and address on the little notepad next to the phone. "The Sunset Hermitage. You know it? Thanks so much. I'll be outside in ten minutes. No, I'm safe at the moment."

"Fanny, please. Just give me a chance to tell you ... show you who I am."

She touched his face and he felt an electrical jolt, as if something had entered his brain. Fanny must have felt it too, because she pulled her hand back and looked carefully at the pathetic, heartbroken man on the bed. There was something about him that made her pause. She had seen the way men looked at women before. Most of the time she'd found, growing up in the brothel, that the lust in their eyes and also betrayed a fear in their hearts, an arrogance and meanness and contempt for women. But Charley wasn't like that. She couldn't tell exactly what it was that made him different. An innocence? A transparency? A softness about his eyes and mouth. She had a great desire to bend down and kiss him full on the lips.

Before either of them could say or do anything, there was a loud thump on the door. The thump in question was so hard that the door shook on its hinges. "Room Service," said a voice with a distinct accent. A loud grunt followed.

"Oh, no," Fanny whispered. "I know that voice. It's him. Charley, we have to get out of here."

"Who? Who are you talking about?" Charley sat up and nearly passed out as the blood left his head.

"I can't tell you now, there's no time. C'mon, Charley. We have to get out." She grabbed his hand and pulled him up just as the door began to creak in its frame from whatever or whoever was pushing against it.

"The window. Quick, it opens into the back garden." Charley flung the window open and Fanny began to climb out. The window was narrow, and Fanny was not. She was halfway through when she got stuck.

"Help me, Charley. I'm stuck. God, I can't move."

"No, you can't be stuck...." Charley began to push her. "Squeeze, Fanny ... squeeze."

"I can't. Push me harder. Hurry!"

Charley had both hands on Fanny's back and his eyes on the door, which was creaking like a ship about to sink. He knew he'd never dislodge her before whoever was trying to get in broke down the door.

"Hang on, Fanny." He jumped over to the bed and began to push it towards the door with a strength he would normally not have had if desperation and potential death hadn't been stimulating his suprarenal glands, producing a level of adrenaline not generally associated with activities in the bedroom. The door, which at that stage was virtually off its hinges, slammed back shut as the heavy bed was jammed up against it. There was a series of awful animal shrieks from the other side and a plea from someone with a slight Irish accent to open the door as they "just wanted to talk."

Charley didn't answer. He tried to think, but he was panicking. Suddenly he had an idea. A pretty stupid one, but an idea nevertheless. Without saying a word to Fanny who was sobbing in frustration, he rushed into the bathroom and grabbed the body lotion. One of the features that the Sunset Hermitage prided itself on was the size and superiority of its bathroom amenities. Charley did not read the side panel of the large bottle, which promised "skin as smooth and sleek as a dolphin" as he pumped and spread huge quantities on Fanny's shoulders and back. As dire as their situation was, he began to get horny as his hands roamed over the vast areas of sensuous skin. He moved his hands down her back to her bottom, which was neither stuck nor bare, but certainly everything he'd fantasized about. His time-sensitive reverie was interrupted by a yell from Fanny as she suddenly slipped from the window frame into a rhododendron bush a few feet below. Charley threw the lotion aside and jumped out. Within seconds they were running through the garden to the lobby.

Stefan Wanke, who clearly had not heard the commotion coming from the isolated garden room, looked up in horror as the two distressed and totally disheveled guests burst through the lobby and out onto the sidewalk in front of the hotel. He rushed from behind the front desk, determined to say something in the strongest possible terms to this degenerate libertine who flaunted the hotel's rules at every opportunity. As Wanke strode toward the front door, he was hit from behind by a large hairy dwarf, followed closely by a tall Italian aristocrat who tripped over him and smashed into a marble statue of a nymph.

The dwarf reached the lobby doors just as a black BMW 5 Series pulled up. He made a frantic dash, but he was too late. Charley and Fanny jumped into the car, which sped off towards Sunset. Nano picked up a heavy glass ashtray and flung it after the BMW. He watched with some satisfaction as it hit an elderly man who was crossing the street with his basset hound.

"My God, Fanny," said Paula as she slowed the car to a more manageable speed. "What the hell's going on and who is this guy?"

"I'm Charley," said Charley from the backseat.

"I never asked you who you were," replied Paula in a voice that sent a chill up Charley's already chilly spine. "I asked Fanny."

"I'm sorry, Paula. That's Charley. He saved my life twice today. We're being chased by some really bad men who want to kill me." Fanny's voice quivered and Charley could sense she was about to break down.

Paula must have sensed it too because she patted Fanny's arm and said, in a soothing voice that contrasted greatly to the harsh threatening tone in which she'd addressed Charley, "Don't say anything more, sweetie. Just breathe and you can tell me everything when we get to my house. And you," she slapped at Charley's hand, which had found its way onto Fanny's shoulder, "you don't say anything at all."

"Yow," said Charley, rubbing his stinging hand. But he said it under his breath.

Ten minutes later they pulled into a drive right below the Hollywood sign. Paula pushed a button on the dash and the wooden gates opened onto what looked to Charlie, in his limited knowledge, like a vintage Hollywood bungalow. She pulled the BMW up to the front door as the gates shut behind them with a reassuring clank, opened the blue front door to the bungalow, and ushered Fanny and Charley into a cozy sitting room. The room was furnished unpretentiously with wood coffee tables, plump couches, and chairs draped in cashmere throws and quilts.

"Sit," ordered Paula, pushing Fanny onto one of the armchairs. "I'm going to get you a drink to help you calm down."

"Um, do you think I might have one too?"

Paula scowled at Charley, and for the first time he was able to get a good look at her. There was something vaguely familiar, but in the bedlam of the night's activities, he couldn't put his finger on it. He sat down on one of the couches and much to his delight Fanny got up from the chair and sat down next to him.

"Charley, I'm so sorry you got caught up in all of this. But I'd be dead if it wasn't for you."

Charley didn't know what to do or say. The sheer proximity to Fanny was playing havoc with his senses. It was if he were about to eat the most delicious thing imaginable. He desperately wanted to take her in his arms, hug her and kiss her, and tell her that he'd do anything for her, but something inside told him that this wasn't the time. The look on Paula's face when she walked out of the kitchen with two cups of what turned out to be hot chocolate confirmed his hesitation.

"Fanny, before you get too cozy with this ... man," she said as if speaking about a worm, "I think we need to find out exactly who he is and why he helped you. Now come and sit over here with me."

Fanny hesitated, then reluctantly stood up and plonked herself down next to Paula on the other couch. She smiled sheepishly at Charley, who felt as if a sudden and awful void had opened up next to him.

"Look here, Paula." Charley summoned up whatever moxie was left in his rapidly depleting supply. "I don't really know who you are either, though you do look somewhat familiar, but clearly we're both trying to help Fanny get away from whoever's chasing her. So why don't you stop threatening me and let's talk like accomplices. Thanks for rescuing us, by the way."

Paula fixed him in a stare that left him in no doubt as to how unintimidating his outburst had been. Then she spoke slowly and deliberately. "First, don't you dare speak to me in that tone again. We are not accomplices and I was rescuing Fanny. I most certainly was not rescuing you. But you're right, I do have Fanny's best interests at heart, and perhaps you do too. I don't know. So tell me exactly who you are and I will decide whether to allow you to stay or to throw you out into the street. And you'd better tell me the truth or I swear you will regret it."

"Okay, Jesus. My name is Charley Brooks, as I told Fanny in the hotel, and I'm a journalist and writer. I was having dinner at the restaurant where Fanny was dancing. As she came onstage two guys rushed her and I just tried to help." He tried to control his voice but Paula's half-closed eyes and grim expression intimidated him.

"It's true, Paula," whispered Fanny, lifting her face from the steaming mug of hot chocolate. "That's exactly how it happened. Then he took me back to his hotel and that's where those other two tried to kill us. I have a really good feeling about Charley. Please don't throw him out."

"Hmm...." Paula stood up and stretched. She was, Charley realized, extremely tall ... no, not just tall, but big ... big like an Amazon. All of a sudden he knew exactly who she was and where he'd seen her. The raven hair. The pale skin. The sinewy arms. Paula was Portia ... Portia, Princess of Pain. The terrible images of Chez Nolan and the Dildo of Doom rushed back into his brain, and he gasped in terror.

Paula spun round. "What? What are you trying to say?"

"No, nothing. I wasn't saying anything. It was just a sigh. Just exhaustion really."

"It didn't sound like a sigh. It sounded like you'd just thought of something. I'm not sure I trust you. It's quite a coincidence that those two were at your hotel, don't you think?"

"I didn't know they were staying at my hotel. Other than the fact that Fanny seems to believe she knows who they are, I have absolutely no clue who they are or what they're up to. Why would they shoot me if I was on their side?"

Paula paused as if considering what to do. "Perhaps. Or perhaps, because it's just a scratch, it was an elaborate ploy."

"Not a ploy. I could have been killed."

"Charley's right, Paula. They were trying to shoot us. I promise. Please don't take it out on him." Fanny sounded almost desperate and Charley's spirits rose.

"Well, I tell you what. I'm sure you're both exhausted so let's leave any further discussion to the morning. You can sleep on the couch and Fanny can share my room. And Fanny, I'm not sure what I've got in my closet that will fit you, but you can't wear that outfit. C'mon, let's go. And you," this to Charley, "I don't want to hear you move in the night. Is that clear?"

"Yes, perfectly. I'll be really quiet."

# CHAPTER 13

Los Angeles, next morning.
*The cold enlightenment of morning.*

Eduardo woke up with a splitting headache. He tried to sit up but the pain was too great, and he felt as if he were going to throw up. He moaned loudly and tried to think back to what had happened just before he'd tripped over the body in the lobby of the Sunset Hermitage and smacked into the marble statue.

"Don't try to get up, Eduardo. You have a bad concussion."

"Bobby?" Eduardo looked over to the doorway, where Bobby Casagrande stood filing his nails. "What happened? I don't remember anything after I hit my head."

"Probably just as well, it was mayhem. That fucking dwarf is out of control. He nearly killed the hotel manager and took out an old guy who was walking his dog. We had to extract both of you before the police arrived. What the hell happened before you hit your head?"

Eduardo blinked his eyes and rubbed his head. His hands encountered what felt like a turban. "What is this?"

"Don't worry, it's just a bandage. You have a cut. Nothing serious and the doctor stitched it. But you have to keep it covered."

"I'm sorry, Bobby, about Nano I mean. I have to call my uncle. He has to do something before Nano gets us all arrested."

"My dad is with Nano now, trying to talk some sense into him."

"I hope he's using the hedge clippers. I'm sure that's the only way he'll listen."

Bobby laughed. "No, they're drinking wine at the pool. I've never seen my dad with a soft spot for anyone, except maybe one of his captains ... but I have to say he certainly has one for the dwarf. I have to get him to tell me why. Anyway, you were saying...."

"I remember being fast asleep when Nano Mortale began to bang on my door and shriek. He pulled me to the window and I saw her—the belly dancer, Fanny, and some man—sneaking through the garden. I put on my clothes and followed Nano through the garden to their room. Nano started trying to force the door. I tried to say we were room service, but that hairy bastard has no patience for subtleties. He began to smash the door in and suddenly we saw them running through the garden to the hotel lobby. They must have jumped through the window. We ran after them and then I tripped. That's as much as I can tell you. I take it we've lost the girl? My uncle will surely kill me now."

"Not yet, my friend. We may have a lead. We had a man outside who saw them get in to a black BMW. He got the license number before they sped off. Would have followed but he thought he should probably stay there to see what happened to you. Which was good thinking, because the manager was about to call in the SWAT team. After our man spoke to him and informed him that you were guests of the Casagrande family, he calmed down."

Eduardo managed to sit up. A wave of nausea hit him, and he closed his eyes until he felt a little better. "I am so sorry this is not going according to plan. And I guess it's all my fault. I should never have allowed the belly dancer to leave without searching her. Or at least checking to see if the book was still there. I'm afraid my uncle is right about me. I am what you would call here in America a loser."

If Eduardo thought he'd get any sympathy from Bobby, he was wrong. Bobby had his own issues. His father had put him in charge of helping the Sabatinis, and so far he'd almost lost two men, and allowed the woman to escape in the chaos of the battle at the Sunset Hermitage. He didn't even know what this "precious" book was all about. How could any book be that valuable?

"Look, Eduardo. I'm in equal shit with my dad. This is the first operation he's put me in charge of, and nothing is going right for me either." Bobby didn't sound as frantic as Eduardo but he was clearly down. "My dad is the head of our family and I'm his only child. At some point, I suppose, he was hoping I'd be his successor, but I doubt he believes that anymore—in fact I'm almost sure he doesn't. My gut feeling is that he'd like to see me vanish, and unless we can get this operation back on track, I imagine that's what's going to happen. And we both know what 'vanish' means...."

Eduardo gave a deep sigh of frustration. This was quite exasperating. He was used to being told what to do and he felt unsure how to react in a situation where he might have to be the more mature party. "Okay, then we are basically, as you say, in the same shit. My uncle, your father, they are just looking for an excuse to get rid of us. We cannot give them any opportunity. So we are going to have to work together. And we have to do so without the dwarf."

"Yeah, but how do we do that? Clearly my father and your uncle trust him more than us. If we're going to do this thing with negotiation rather than violence, we need to find a way to get rid of the little bastard. So if you have any ideas, now would be the time."

"Maybe we could get him really drunk. Then we tie a rock from the garden to his legs and drown him in the swimming pool...."

Bobby shrugged. "Really? You can see the two of us doing that? Look, I hate violence, Eduardo, and I suspect you do too. Though that isn't really a good trait in our line of work. Here...." He handed Eduardo a cup of coffee and a couple of Advil.

"Well, this isn't exactly my first choice when it comes to work," Eduardo said, swallowing the Advil with a sip of the coffee. He managed to sit up slowly. "I would rather be an actor."

"An actor? You probably should have been born a Barrymore rather than a Sabatini. Although, you know what, I guess I could see you as an actor. You have that European charm. You ever done it before?"

"No, I've never done anything before. My parents were killed when I was six years old and my Uncle Bruno, the marchese, was put in charge of my up-bringing, which he did with the least amount of affection and a good deal of violence. Not that I saw much of him. He hired an Irish governess to take care of me. She was not a nice person. Very cruel. In fact, I have nightmares still thinking about that evil bitch. I did kill her eventually, which helped a bit."

"Jesus, I thought you weren't into violence?"

"I'm not really, and I didn't feel all that good about killing her. But I had no choice. So I don't count it."

"I don't get it."

"Well, in our family it is a tradition for the son to bloody his hands at some point before his eighteenth birthday. You have to kill something you love. She was the obvious choice."

"Now, I'm totally confused. You say you hated her and now you say you loved her...."

"It's complicated, Bobby. For me love and hate are the same thing. I love the things I hate. Maybe I'll tell you about it at some point. But not now."

Bobby stood up from the edge of Eduardo's bed and walked over to the window. He could see his father on a chaise at the pool still having an animated conversation with Nano, who had climbed into a tree.

"Look, I can see only one way to take care of Nano. I have some stuff I can get hold of."

Eduardo got out of bed rather gingerly. His head felt a little better from the Advil and the nausea had gone away after the coffee. He took Bobby's hand and shook it. For the first time in days he felt a lessening of the tension that had only exacerbated his throbbing head. This would be a partnership. Something he had never experienced before. He had a good feeling about working with Bobby. At least he had no apparent desire to cut Eduardo's throat or squeeze his head till it popped open like an overripe pomegranate.

Within the hour Nano had drunk the bottle of wine that Bobby had given him in three large gulps. He didn't notice the taste of chloral hydrate and was soon snoring gently on one of the chaises at the pool. The don, who was certainly inebriated from the large quantities of wine he'd drunk with Nano prior to the doctored bottle, had wandered off to do some topiary. He was in the midst of shaping a particularly uncooperative privet into a kangaroo when an awful shriek from the pool area caused him to topple off the ladder. He staggered over to find the butler cursing like a lunatic and covered in fecal matter. Then he saw Nano. It didn't seem possible that anyone could have had that much shit in them. He yelled for Bobby and Eduardo to help him, but they seemed to have vanished. So he grabbed a garden hose and set to work.

Charley woke up in slightly better shape than Eduardo had. His head was still sore from his encounter with the fire extinguisher, and his arm throbbed from where the bullet had grazed him, but all in all, considering the chaos of the past two days, he felt okay. He thought about Fanny and wondered if she was still sleeping in the bedroom with Paula. For a second and a half he conjured up a vision of Paula and Fanny together, but forced it from his mind before his libido had an opportunity to respond. He had no wish to find out what Paula would do to him if she discovered anything unusual on her couch. The door was shut, so he pulled the blanket up over his head and tried to sleep. But it was impossible. There were too many synapses firing in his brain. He was both thrilled and terrified. He'd found Fanny but he had absolutely no idea what to do next. So he closed his eyes and tried to meditate.

"Charley, wake up. I've made you some coffee."

Perhaps it was the pale morning sun that had crept into the sitting room, bathing Fanny in a soft glow that turned her thick red hair to molten copper, or perhaps it was simply the cataclysmic nature of the situation playing tricks with Charley's mind, but at that moment he believed that he was in the presence of someone who was not of this world. He felt himself melting, turning into butter, as if her face was the sun. He smiled up at her and she kissed him on the lips. It was not a long kiss. It was not a full kiss. Tongues did not touch. And yet it was a kiss more passionate and fuller than Charley had ever experienced. In that brief moment, when her lips brushed his, something changed in Charley, but at the time he did not know what it was.

"What the hell is going on here?" Paula said, becoming Portia. She was dressed in a skintight black leotard that showed off her incredibly tight, muscular body. Fanny stood up and laughed. She was dressed, Charley saw, in a pair of stretch pants that would have been tight on Paula, and a sweatshirt that, as baggy as it was, could not hide her joyful breasts no longer held in place by the tasseled top from last night.

"It's okay, Paula. I was just kissing Charley good morning. C'mon, Charley. You have to get up." She pulled the blanket from him and giggled.

"Really? By the look of him he's already up. Christ, men are disgusting."

Charley grabbed the blanket back from Fanny and tried desperately to hide his erection. Fanny giggled again. "That's so sweet."

"Don't be so naïve, Fanny. That's not sweet at all. Trust me, I've dealt with people like him. You," she pointed at Charley, "take your filthy erection to the guest bathroom—the first door on the left—and you'd better not leave the seat up. You're going to have to shower and get dressed quickly. Then you have to go."

Charley wrapped the blanket around his waist and stood up. "Look, Por ... uh, Paula. I'm not leaving Fanny. It's too dangerous."

"I know that, and that's why the two of you are leaving together. I have no doubts that whoever's after you will probably trace my plates, someone will remember them believe me, and they'll come looking for you."

Charley took a sip of his coffee and shuffled off to the bathroom with his clothes from the previous evening. He too, he realized, would have to get some new clothes. He couldn't go back to the Sunset Hermitage that was for sure. As he peed, he looked out the window and saw the black BMW. There was nothing unusual about it except for the license plate, which simply said PAIN.

# CHAPTER 14

Los Angeles, later that same morning.
*The cost of taking the freeway.*

When he walked back into the sitting room after his shower, he found Paula and Fanny looking at a map of what appeared to be the western United States.

"Where are we going?" Charley asked, as Paula traced a route with a red felt-tip pen.

Fanny looked up at him and smiled. "Paula's tracing the route from Los Angeles to Worland."

"Worland? I don't know where that is."

"It's in Wyoming. Where my mom lives. And she has the book."

"Fanny, I have no idea what you're talking about. What book?"

"Oh, Charley. You're right, I haven't really told you anything, have I?"

"Fanny, stop." Paula becoming Portia said as she slammed the red pen down. "Before you tell this man anything more, I need to know why he's helping you. I know you think he's saved your life, but he's not doing it for the sake of doing it. He wants something. All men do."

Charley sat down in the armchair and rubbed his forehead. The bump seemed like it was going down. He wanted to tell them everything. He wanted to talk about *Porky Asses* and the Nolans and how he knew Paula was Portia, but he just couldn't. Fanny, Paula, and he were all dancing around the truth, and he was the only one who knew it. So Charley leaned back, crossed his legs, and began to talk.

"There's obviously a lot I haven't told you about my life. Neither have you two, for that matter. Though we haven't exactly had much time together. But I will tell everything about me so that you know that there isn't anything I want except to help Fanny."

Fanny opened her mouth, but Paula stopped her. "Okay, so you've said you're a writer and you told us how you saw Fanny. But why do you want to help her? Why don't you want to call the cops? What are you hiding, Charley Brooks?"

"Well I didn't say I didn't want to call the cops, and we can if you think they'll help us escape from whoever is chasing us. I'm not hiding anything about myself. I'm not some dangerous criminal on the most-wanted list or anything like that. You can look me up ... I'm a writer and a journalist. I used to be a war correspondent. I came to Los Angeles because my fiancée dumped me. I have to admit I was feeling pretty shitty until I saw Fanny in the restaurant. I'm not sure what it was, but something happened. I told her in the hotel, something snapped inside me. I know that sounds weird but it did, and I can't help it.

I'm not sure what the feeling is exactly ... there, that's it. That's all I can say."

Fanny stood up and walked over to Charley. She leaned down and kissed him on the forehead. She didn't say anything, but she didn't need to. The strange whomp he'd felt when she'd kissed him earlier reverberated around his head, and somehow he knew she'd felt it too.

"Hmm," said Paula, looking over at them. "You know what, I believe you. I've seen men in stressful situations before and I know when I'm being lied to."

*I bet you have*, Charley wanted to say. His mind whirling back to the horrific photos on Mrs. Nolan's desk. *And you've been the main cause of those stressful situations, Portia or Paula or whatever your real name is*. But he lowered his eyes and said nothing.

"So here's the plan. Charley. You have to get Fanny back to Worland, and you have to get the damn book back that these guys want so badly."

"What is this mysterious book?" Charley interrupted.

"I wish I knew," said Fanny. "I took it from Eduardo's desk because he wouldn't pay me. I put it in my bag and only thought about it when I got to Los Angeles. But it's all I took, so that's what they must be after."

"Must be a first edition of some sort. And a really valuable one at that. How old was it?"

"I don't know, but it has to be pretty old. It looks more like one of those illuminated manuscripts that monks used to illustrate. Though I have to say the illustrations depict some things monks should not have much knowledge of. I literally took a quick glance and put it in my bag. I couldn't read any of it, but if anything I would say it was a codex."

"I don't even know what a codex is," said Paula.

"The first bound manuscripts that replaced papyrus rolls," Fanny said dismissively, almost as if it was something she was forced to explain every day. "Some of them are pretty mysterious, like the Voynich codex or the Rohonc."

Charley listened as Fanny gave a concise and, from what he understood about codices, accurate description. He realized with some degree of embarrassment that he hadn't given Fanny's mental capacity quite as much attention as he'd given her physical allure. Her explanation of the various hypotheses surrounding the Rohonc Codex made him realize that her mind was formidable, and he felt ashamed of himself for not having considered that she was more than simply stunning.

"Anyway," she concluded, unaware of Charley's self-imposed humiliation, "I sent it with some other stuff I'd bought in Rome to my mother in Worland. But then they found me in the restaurant, and now they're after me and I've got you involved, and I don't know what to do."

"Slow down, sweetie. None of this is going to make sense to him. Just tell him everything you told me last night. But my gut feel is you should be quick. They're going to find my car soon, I know it. In any case, I have an appointment in ninety minutes."

Charley took Fanny's hand and squeezed it reassuringly as she began to relate the story from when Eduardo's assistant had recruited her after her agent had placed an advert in a belly dancing magazine. She left nothing out other than her photo session for *Porky Asses*, though she did mention she'd had to do some plus-size modeling to make extra money.

"Jesus," said Charley after she'd finished. "Do you know who the Sabatini Family are?"

"No, only that Eduardo seemed nice, though he wouldn't pay me for my time. That's why I took the book, Charley. It was payment."

"You should have kneed him in his balls, Fanny. That's the only thing men like that understand."

Charley winced. "Actually, good thing you didn't. Eduardo Sabatini is the nephew of the current Don. He may be nice, but the Sabatinis are one of the oldest, richest, nastiest, most ruthless crime families in Italy. Their trail of murder, theft, blackmail, kidnapping literally goes back hundreds of years. The legend is that just about every crime family in the world, other than the Chinese tongs and Japanese Yakuza, got their start with the Sabatinis." Charley squeezed Fanny's hand a little tighter. "Whatever the book is that you took from them, they obviously want it back rather badly, and they aren't going to just let you off lightly. I would bet they're over here working with one of the local mob families to find you ... to find us. I'm in it with you, Fanny. I promise. I'm not going to leave you. But we have to realize the danger."

"Jesus, he is right," Paula pursed her lips and exhaled. "That's really screwed up. Do you think they'll call things off if they get the book back?"

"I don't know. All we can do is try. The question is how do we contact them and ask?"

"I'm so sorry, Paula and Charley. I really messed up. I can't let you get more involved."

"First of all, you didn't mess up," said Paula. "Well, you did a bit by taking the book I suppose, but they could just have asked for it back instead of trying to kill you. Second, don't worry about me. I can take care of myself. It's you we have to worry about, and now this guy." She pointed a long threatening finger at Charley.

"Hey, listen. I've been in bad situations before. Not exactly with Italian mafiosos, it's true, but I can't imagine they're any worse than Congolese guerillas drunk on palm wine. So don't underestimate me. I promise you I' know how to handle myself...."

Fanny smiled. Paula rolled her eyes and groaned.

"Please," she said, "we don't need stories of your heroics. What we need is a plan. So unless you have something vaguely intelligent to say, be quiet."

Charley, still flushed from underestimating Fanny, let it slide. Then he thought of something. "You know, maybe there is a way to get a message to some of the local mob families."

"How?"

"I'm going to call a friend of mine. A reporter at the *Los Angeles Times* who focuses on organized crime. I would bet he has some connections. Even if he can just give them my mobile phone number and get them to contact us somewhere on the road."

Paula and Fanny nodded in agreement and Charley took out his flip phone, one of the few things besides his wallet that he hadn't left at the hotel. He called his friend, who was fortunately at his desk, and after numerous warnings about what the mobsters were capable of doing and how there was new technology that might allow them to trace his phone while he was on the road, his friend reluctantly agreed to put out some feelers and call him back as soon as he had anything of substance.

Then Paula, offering to lend them one of her cars, led them out the kitchen to the garage, where a vehicle was covered in a large tarpaulin. In one swift movement, she tugged it aside.

Charley nearly wet himself. "Paula, this is an amazing car."

"I'm not into cars, so I have no idea."

Charley walked around the convertible Mustang and whistled. "This is a brand-new SVT Cobra. Are you serious? You'll lend this to us? Really, this is unbelievable. How did you get one of these babies?"

"Not that it's your business, but it was a gift from a client."

"I bet he was a very satisfied client," Charley said, though he regretted it almost immediately. Paula became Portia once again. She walked up to him slowly and gripped his shoulder tightly. Then she dug her fingers into the nerve endings with such intensity that he almost screamed. "Ow, Jesus. Why'd you do that?"

"Because you were rude and rude people get punished." She let go of his arm and immediately reverted to Paula. "It's very fast and it's manual so I can't drive it anyway."

"Neither can I," said Fanny. "I'm awful with stick shift."

"Well, I'm not," Charley said. "It's how I learned to drive."

Paula tossed him the keys. "Good then, you drive and Fanny can navigate."

Fanny grabbed Paula and gave her a hug. "Paula, this is wonderful. I promise we'll look after it and get it back to you."

"I know you will, sweetie. That's one thing I'm not worried about. Look, I have to prepare for a client, so be safe and call me when you can." She put her arms around Fanny and kissed her full on the lips. Then she gestured from her eyes to Charley with her index and middle finger to let him know she was watching him.

They got into the car, which roared to life as soon as Charley turned the ignition. Paula moved the BMW and opened the gate for them, and they pulled out of the house and onto the quiet street. Ten minutes later they realized that in their excitement they'd left the map on the coffee table.

"Don't worry about, it," said Charley. "I have a great sense of direction."

Shortly after that they got horribly lost.

# CHAPTER 15

Los Angeles, 30 minutes later.
*Doms are scarier than Dons.*

"I think that must be the house over there ... that old Hollywood Bungalow."

Bobby had pulled his white XJS convertible into a parking spot a few doors down from Paula's house. He and Eduardo were sipping coffee they'd picked up at a Starbucks, and rapidly coming to the realization that good intentions do not constitute a plan.

Finally, Eduardo made a decision. "Look, Bobby, if she is there ... if Fanny is in the house, then I believe I must go in alone and try to talk her into giving back the book. She knows me and she won't be scared. I will offer her money. A great deal of money if I have to." He reached up to his head, which was still wrapped in the bandage. "I should take this off in case it scares her."

"Don't do that," said Bobby, pulling Eduardo's hand away. "The stitches will scare her even more. Just be yourself. We know the woman who owns the BMW. Her name is Paula Cockburn, and she has 'model' listed as her profession on her license application. But we know what that really means."

"You think she is a call girl?"

"Of course. Probably one of those very expensive ones that cost a grand for half an hour. So don't worry, she's not going to be a threat. It's the guy with them, maybe her pimp, that might be dangerous. Just offer a lot of money. That's what these people want."

"Perhaps, my dear friend. I will be careful, but I will be deadly if necessary. You can see the front door from here. If I need help, and I am sure I won't, I will raise both hands like this, and you can come help me. But I have a feeling this is going to be peaceful and pleasant." Eduardo pulled a rolled-up wad of money out his pocket and flicked through it. The he got out the car and walked to the gate. He felt a little less sure of himself when he saw the black BMW in the driveway. He stopped and began to breath heavily as if he were about to experience a panic attack. He swallowed, gulped, made a fist, and steeled himself. This was his chance to prove to his uncle that he was capable of doing something right.

Bobby watched Eduardo make his way to the house. He started strong, with a definite spring in his step, but the closer he got to the door, the less confident he seemed to become. Bobby hoped more than anything that Eduardo would not have to signal for help. The closest thing he had to a weapon was an old golf umbrella in the trunk. He was also a little nervous that the bandage wound round Eduardo's head would unnerve Fanny. It hadn't worried him at first when Eduardo suggested removing it, but the more he looked at the now quaking figure about to knock on the door, the more he felt that the turbanlike bandage made Eduardo look like the bashi-bazouk his father had once shown him in a book to terrify him.

There was a narrow window to the side of the door and Eduardo peered in, hoping to see a trace of Fanny. All he could make out in the front room were couches and chairs and a coffee table on which rested what looked like an open map. He clenched his buttocks, raised his hand, hesitated a few times, then knocked on the door.

Perhaps if it had been a hard knock, the kind of knock police make just before doing a drug bust, the events that followed would have been less painful. But it was a soft knock. A timid knock. The kind of knock employed by those who'd made a private appointment to be corrected by Portia, Princess of Pain.

Eduardo was about to knock again when the door was flung open and a woman more terrifying than any he'd ever seen filled the door frame. Two things went through his mind before the Amazonlike creature, dressed in form-fitting black leather, kicked him behind the knees and flung him to the ground. The first was that his darkest fantasy involving powerful women was about to become reality. The second, as the woman's whip slashed him across his back, was that it would be a good deal more painful in reality than it had been in his imagination.

Portia had been in her bedroom putting the finishing touches to her costume when she heard the knock. She was very annoyed. How many times must she impress on her clients that on time means on time? Not a minute before and not a minute after. Well, this miserable specimen wouldn't make the same mistake again. She had fastened the utility belt containing sprays, lubes, and odd-looking sexual accouterment around her waist, grabbed a nasty-looking whip, and strode off to the door. She caught a glimpse of the man outside. She didn't remember her agent telling her that her client was Indian. She doubted the full head-mask would fit over his turban, and that annoyed her even more. She hated compromise.

"How dare you arrive early?

"I'm so sorry, I think there's been ... yeow!"

"Shut up, you miserable piece of excrement. I did not give you permission to talk." Portia gave the man squirming under the six-inch stiletto she had strategically placed between his shoulder blades another whack with her whip.

"Please," begged Eduardo, "you don't understand. I want to go...."

"No," whispered Portia into his ear as she clapped handcuffs onto his wrist, "you don't understand. You paid for an hour of suffering and you're going to get an hour of suffering."

"But I didn't...." Eduardo's pleas were cut off as a red ball-gag was shoved into his mouth. The bandage on his head had come loose and was falling over his eyes, making vision all but impossible. Portia grabbed his right ear and pulled him up into a standing position. She prodded him with the whip towards a door that led downstairs into a basement bathed in an eerie red light. Through the rapidly detangling bandage, Eduardo could make out an array of what looked like medieval torture devices. Fear and confusion yielded to arousal, and he felt himself regress to a much younger man in the hands of a demented ex-nun.

Portia didn't realize her mistake until thirty-five minutes into the session. Her patient had yelled and squealed a great deal. But that was normal in these sessions. It was the hot wax, explicitly specified in his written request, that pushed him over the edge. Eduardo, his pants and boxers pulled off and lying in a heap on the floor, was tied to a bench when Portia poured it onto his balls. She removed the handcuffs and examined him carefully. He'd stopped jerking about like a landed trout about ten minutes before and he was staring at her with wide terrified eyes. It was not the normal expression of someone who got off on extreme pain. She pulled the gag out his mouth and he began to blabber like an idiot. She couldn't understand him. It sounded like he was speaking a foreign language.

"What's your safe word?" she hissed with just a top-note of uncertainty.

"Gesu, Giuseppe, Maria," whimpered Eduardo.

"No, I don't recognize that one," Portia responded.

"Cagna Pazza!" he yelled, recovering a bit of his sanity. But Portia didn't recognize the Italian for 'crazy bitch' as a safe word either, so she poured a little more wax onto his scalded balls. So great was the pain that Eduardo leapt up and, battering the Princess of Pain aside with his head, made a dash for the staircase. By the time Portia had recovered he was out the door, rushing towards a white Jaguar with nothing but a map he'd grabbed off the coffee table to cover his severely injured genitals.

"Holy fuck," said Bobby, trying not to stare at Eduardo's horribly red and extremely painful-looking balls as he maneuvered the Jaguar down Laurel Canyon to Sunset. "Those bastards! Why did they torture you? What did they want?"

"I don't know. Dolce Madre di Dio, but my balls hurt. There was only one of them. She looked like a woman, but she had the strength of Nano. And she was magnificent, Bobby. Very hurtful but truly fantastic."

"So what did you find out?"

"All she wanted to know was why I was early, and what kind of safe I had."

"What kind of safe you have? That doesn't make sense. Do you think the kind of safe you kept the book in?"

"I honestly don't know, Bobby. But she asked me twice. Now, please. We have to stop at a pharmacy. I need to get something for the pain before I pass out."

Bobby nodded and pulled into a strip mall where there was a Rite Aid Pharmacy. "Don't be too long," he said as he parked the car. "We're going to have to tell my father."

"What do you mean 'don't be too long'? How do expect me to go in like this without any pants?"

"Okay, I suppose you're right. Well, wait here then and think of something we can tell my dad. He's going to be fucking insane."

Bobby was back five minutes later with some aloe vera gel that the pharmacist had recommended for sunburn. He tossed the bottle to Eduardo, who squirted it liberally on his testicles and began to rub them furiously. Bobby almost threw up as he turned the car out of the parking lot.

"Stay in the car and I'll go in and get you some pants," said Bobby as they pulled up at the Casagrande compound. "And for God's sake, keep that map over your crotch until I come back in case one of the guards looks in."

Eduardo watched Bobby go into the house before he lifted the map gingerly and examined himself. The aloe vera had definitely helped with the pain, though not with the 'evil thoughts,' as his governess would have said, that raged through his mind. The hot wax had caused him a great deal of suffering. More than the sharp spurs of the old contessa in Luca, or the nipple clamps of the family courtesan Bella Castiglione. Or god forbid, the hairbrush of his late governess. And yet he could not stop thinking of Portia and he knew, more than anything else, that he had to see her again.

He absentmindedly tugged at a large dollop of the hardened wax. The pain was excruciating as the wax came away, taking his scrotal hair with it. He wanted to scream in both agony and frustration. When were things going to go right for once? Tears filled his eyes and a great sadness came over him. He looked down again, and for the first time noticed that someone had drawn on the map that strategically covered his nakedness. He picked it and examined it closely. It showed a highlighted route from Los Angeles to a town in Wyoming called Worland. By the time Bobby walked up holding a pair of loose-fitting gym shorts, Eduardo had remembered exactly what it was about Wyoming that struck him as familiar. Suddenly he felt that his and Bobby's luck was about to change.

# CHAPTER 16

Between Los Angeles and Worland.
*Love is hard but worth the struggle.*

The good news for Charley was that Fanny didn't seem to be getting upset at his lack of any sense of direction. She seemed totally enthralled by his stories of his days as a war correspondent, and once again he found himself marveling at her broad understanding of foreign policy. Sitting next to her in the warm California sun made him happier than he imagined he'd been at any point in his life. All he wanted to do was take her in his arms and hold her. Well, at least as a first step. But as his mind raced through the myriad sensations and possibilities that now presented themselves, he began to question whether he'd ever really loved before.

Charley's problem was that he jumped into relationships headfirst, and he did so easily and often. At the age of seven he'd fallen head-over-heels for Rosy Alfheim, the daughter of their next-door neighbor. Rosy, as her name suggested, was blond and blue-eyed with big red apple-cheeks, and thought Charley was the funniest person she'd ever met. Both sets of parents thought it was the sweetest thing imaginable, until Charley stole a pack of his father's Marlboros so that he and Rosy could pretend to be real cowboys. Two puffs into their second cigarettes they were caught by Rosy's mother, and the relationship ended.

During his freshman year at Northwestern, Charley had begun to read the great romantic poets. His dark curly hair gave him the appearance of a latter-day Lord Byron, and in what he believed was the spirit of the degenerate poet, he began to invite women to go with him to sit on the rocky shore of Lake Michigan in the early evenings. Here he'd read them poetry he'd composed and ply them with champagne. Then in a wild gesture reminiscent of the aristocrat on the edge of the Ionian Sea, he'd toss his glass into the cold dark water, present the young lady with a single red rose, and declare his undying love. It may have worked slightly better if Charley had Byron's virtuosity, and had not the cost of champagne glasses and roses taken its toll on his allowance.

There were flings and longer-term relationships through adulthood, but nothing that Charley considered serious until he met Alexandra. She was the first person he believed he could share his life with had fate, in the form of Fanny, not intervened.

"Charley, Charley! Earth to Charley!" Fanny yelled, putting her hand on his thigh and almost causing him to lose control of the car. "Where exactly are we going?"

Charley's heart sank. "Do you mean the two of us?"

"Yes, of course, the two of us. I'm right here next to you. But you're taking us in exactly the opposite direction of where we should be going...."

"Uh, I am? We are? I think we're headed north."

"No, this is Anaheim. Look, you can see Disneyland."

"You can? Yes, I guess you're right. I'm a total idiot. We should have gone back for the map."

"No, you're not, and I don't care about being lost. There's no real hurry to get anywhere, is there?"

"Hopefully not, but we don't know. We should probably give Por ... uh, Paula a call and see if anyone has visited her place. I'm a little worried."

"I don't think you need to worry about Paula," Fanny said with a slight giggle. "She's usually the one that other people worry about. But I do have to pee, and we need to get clothes. So why don't you pull into that gas station? I'll call her, you get a map and ask where the Walmart is."

Charley pumped the gas while Fanny performed her ablutions and then he gave her his cellphone while he went in to pay and inquire about the nearest Walmart.

As the clerk ran his credit card for the gas and the map, Charley looked out the window at Fanny, who seemed to be laughing hysterically at something Paula was telling her. Obviously, everything was okay.

"That your missus?" asked the clerk, pointing at Fanny who was leaning over the car as she talked.

"Um, well we're traveling together, if that's what you mean?"

"Oh, I don't mean anything ... I jus wanna know if you is together, 'cause I ain't seen an ass like that in my life. And if you ain't with her, I'm gonna get me a piece of it."

"No, you're fucking well not," said Charley, taking the map. "You keep your filthy paws to yourself. How dare you?"

"How dare I? I'll fuckin' show you how I dare. I'm gonna sneak up behind her and grab it. That's how a real man would act. You're obviously not good enough for a woman like that." The clerk was almost drooling. "I'm telling you she needs a real man, and that's jus what I am. A real red-blooded American man."

"No, you're a real moron, and if you take one step towards her, I'll shove the hose right up your ass and light a match. How does that grab you?" Charley stormed out of the kiosk, completely forgetting to ask about the Walmart. But he was worried. Was the 'Fanny Effect' contagious? Would other men be as smitten by her as the gas station attendant was? If he needed further confirmation of that worry, he got it as he walked up to the car. Fanny was still on the phone, bent over the hood of the car and displaying her bottom to anyone who cared to look. Every man at the gas station had his eyes focused on what Junior Nolan had called "the woman who put the Ass in Class." Charley glared at the gawkers and rushed over to Fanny, who stood up and closed the phone.

"Quick," said Charley. "We need to get out of here before someone gets too interested in you ... in us. You don't know how these mobsters get their info.

Any of these people could be a one of their goons."
He gunned the car out of the gas station and immediately realized he had no idea in which direction to
head.

"Is this the way to the Walmart?"

"Uh, yes, I think this is the way the clerk said to
go." But of course it wasn't, and they drove around for
another ten minutes.

"You're the worst, Charley. Look, it's all the way
over there. You're hopeless at direction. I think you'd
better give me the map when we get to the parking
lot."

A few minutes later, after a rapid U-turn in which
they narrowly missed being hit by a bus, they pulled
into the Walmart parking lot. As Charley was about
to get out of the car, he noticed that Fanny had suddenly lowered her head and put her hands up to her
face.

"What's wrong, Fanny. Are you okay?"

"Oh, Charley. I just called you 'the worst' but I'm
such an idiot. I don't have any money. I didn't even
think about it. I'm so sorry."

"Not a problem," he replied, taking her hand. "I never thought you had a wallet concealed in your belly
dancing outfit. I'm going to pay. Now, I know you're
going to protest, so don't even try. I promise you I've
got the money and I want to do it. Although, you
know, we can go to somewhere better than Walmart."

"No, Walmart's perfect for what we need." She smiled at him. "And you can pay on one condition: you let
me pay you back when we get to my momma's house
in Worland."

"Fine, but let's not even think about it now. Let's just go in and get what we need."

Walmart, as Fanny predicted, was indeed perfect for everything they needed. And if Charley was disappointed when Fanny refused to let him be there when she chose underwear, he didn't show it. No because he wasn't interested, he most definitely was, but rather because he was too busy making sure that no one was observing them too closely. The good news about Walmart was that half the people in the store were bursting out of their clothes and more focused on what they were buying than their fellow shoppers. A big scruffy man with a mop of unbrushed hair and a large, stunningly beautiful redheaded belly dancer hardly stood out at all.

They managed to fit everything they'd bought into two small duffels and were soon barreling along the 15 towards Victorville on what Fanny said was the quickest way to get to Worland.

"What did Paula say?" asked Charley. "She didn't get any unusual visitors asking about us, I'm assuming?"

"No, just some Indian guy in a turban who apparently didn't really know what he was doing there. She said he ran out without his pants but took the map to cover himself."

"And that's not unusual?"

"Oh, Charley. You do know what Paula does, don't you?"

"I do not. Not a clue, I'm afraid." he replied, possibly too emphatically.

"She's a dominatrix. She does all sorts of things to men who feel they need to be punished. I don't really get it...."

"Good grief, no. Sounds weird to me too." Charley realized that he was slipping into dangerous territory, and his imagination, which was starting to go into a dark place, would have to be controlled. "So the Indian guy was a regular client?"

"No, that's why I was laughing. He was at the wrong address. Her regular client arrived about ten minutes after the Indian ran out with the map."

"That doesn't sound right, Fanny. I'm a little worried, I have to say. I wish my friend at the LA Times would call back."

"Oh, God, I'm sorry, Charley. He did call while you were paying for gas. He asked me to tell you to call him."

"That's a pity," he said, trying to sound as calm as he could so as not to upset Fanny even more, but she sensed the frustration in his voice and her lower lip quivered.

"Hey, hey," he said touching her shoulder. Don't worry, Fanny, we've only lost an hour. Please don't get upset, I'm sure it's fine."

"No, it's not, Charley. And you have every right to be mad at me. I've done nothing but mess everything up all along the way. I'm such a klutz." She began to cry in earnest. Charley moved his hand from her shoulder to her thigh, which he patted gently. But Fanny's emotions had progressed beyond the calming nature of a gentle pat. Her sobs became wails and then the floodgates opened to full capacity, let-

ting loose a torrent of tears and snot beyond anything Charley had ever experienced. He felt as if his
heart would break seeing her in such anguish, and so
he pulled the car over to the side of the road and took
her, as best he could in the cramped conditions, into his arms. He kissed her cheek, trying to avoid the
proboscil discharge, and much to his rapidly growing
euphoria she responded.

She put her hands up to his face and drew him
up so that their lips touched. It was the briefest of
kisses. Lips moving over lips. The tips of tongues tas-
ting each other for but a second. And yet it was both
fiery and passionate, and a delicious pain flooded
Charley's body, making him feel that he was about to
drown. It became both his joy and his torment because it reinforced his inability to comprehend what
it was that had happened. What had drawn him to
this empyrean being who made his nerves jump every time he looked at her? He had no clue. All he knew
was that he wanted more. But more would have to
wait until they had a larger space in which to take
things to stage two.

"Fanny, whatever happened, we can deal with it.
You are the most amazing thing to ever happen to
me."

"I am? Well, after everything that's happened it's
hard to believe. But I think I feel the same way about
you, Charley"

As Charley was about to ask her what she meant
by 'think,' she kissed him again. And then again and
again, and just when Charlie felt his whole body

would burst like a ripe cantaloupe, his phone rang. It was his friend from the LA *Times*.

"Charley, what the hell, man? Why didn't you call me back?

Charley untangled himself from Fanny, who appeared to have gone into some trancelike state. "Mike, I'm so sorry. I didn't get your message until a few minutes ago. Did you find anything out?"

"As a matter of fact, I did. And I have a response for you."

"Good? Bad?"

"Well, just as you thought, the Sabatinis are working with the most powerful mob family here in Los Angeles, the Casagrandes. I spoke to my contact, who's a minor capo with the Casagrande organization, and it's not good, pal. How the fuck did you get caught up in this?"

"That's a long story which I will tell you over a few beers one of these days."

"Hopefully you'll still be around for 'one of these days.' No, these guys are out to get you. You have the nephew of the head of the Sabatini family working hand in hand with Bobby Casagrande, son of the local don. My contact says you don't have much to worry about with them—they're major disappointments to their families—but you do have to worry about Nano Mortale."

"Who's he?"

"Nano Mortale is the most mentally disturbed hit man on this fucking planet... Nano Mortale... the Deadly Dwarf. The guy is an animal, Charley, and his orders are to get back whatever you have...."

"We want to give it back to him...."

"And then he, and the Casagrande enforcer, Sammy "Peppers" Giardiniera, will kill you and your belly dancer in an unbelievably excruciating manner."

"Oh, Jesus. What do we do?"

"I don't exactly know, Charley. All I can think of is for you to get whatever it is they want and get it back to them. Then get the hell out the country to somewhere they'll never find you, wherever that may be."

"What about the cops, Mike? Do you think I can go to them?

"These guys work with the cops. They're probably the ones who will track you on your way to Worland."

"Did you just say Worland? How do they know we're going to Worland?

"Apparently they have a map detailing your trip. You must have left it somewhere."

# CHAPTER 17

The Casagrande compound, Los Angeles.
*"You got balls" is not always a compliment.*

"Jesus," said Freddy "Six Fingers" when he saw Eduardo hobbling into the house wearing a pair of Bobby's high school gym shorts and what was left of his turbanlike bandage. "Where the hell were you guys? It's been a shit storm around here. And I mean that literally. That fucking dwarf just about exploded after that Lambrusco you gave him, Bobby."

"That's terrible," Bobby replied, trying to sound concerned. "Is he okay?"

"He's fine now. But I wouldn't go near the pool for a few days until we can get the hazmat guys in." The don had a coldness to his voice that Eduardo hadn't heard before.

"I'm sorry, Pops. But we had a horrific experience too."

"Well, uh, Bobby," said Eduardo, sitting down in one of the big armchairs, "I think your experience was perhaps a little less horrific than mine."

"Okay, Eduardo. I take your point. Anyway, while you and Nano were drinking wine, Pops, I got a call from one of our guys saying they'd traced the plates of the BMW to a woman who lived in the Hollywood Hills. Me and Eduardo paid her a visit. Eduardo went in first thinking he may be able to speak to the belly dancer. But they were waiting for him. Tortured him badly, but he escaped and, here's the good part, he picked up a map."

"Whoa, hold on there, boys," said the Don, who was trying desperately not to stare at Eduardo's blistered balls, which had snuck out the side of the too-short gym shorts when he sat down. "None of this makes sense. Who tortured you? Why did they torture you? And what could you tell them? We are the ones who are going to do the torturing."

"You are right, Don Casagrande. None of it made sense. The woman who was torturing me...."

"A woman? A single woman?"

"Yes, but you have never encountered such a woman. Strong, like you have never seen. Powerful, like you have never felt. And beautiful, beyond compare...."

"Sounds as if you are attracted to her," said the Don, getting more agitated by Eduardo's testicles, which seemed to have abandoned the shorts completely and were draped on his beautiful white chair.

"Well, you know, Don Casagrande, one of the things I learned from our Chicago friends is that a deep relationship often develops between the torturer and the torturee."

"Enough," said the Don, who was about to vomit. "Just tell me what she wanted and what is this map."

Eduardo looked slightly crestfallen. Talking openly about his ordeal had cleared his head and helped him understand the weird need he suddenly had to see Portia again. Bobby, sensing his friend was going nowhere with the story, jumped in. "She wanted to know what brand of safe we had? We think she believes the book is in a safe?"

"But the other woman has the book, the fat one. We want the book. Why would we have it in a safe?"

"Fat is not the right word to describe Fanny," Eduardo corrected Don Casagrande. "She is large, that is true. But her flesh is firm and supple. There is nothing fat about her." He looked down suddenly and saw his protruding appendages, which he hurriedly grabbed and shoved back in his shorts. "Merda," he yelped, "my balls are killing me."

"I'll fucking kill you if they pop out again and you don't tell me what this map is."

Bobby jumped in once more. "It's a map we believe the belly dancer and her male companion are following to her mother's house in Wyoming. The route is marked, and Eduardo remembers her telling him that her mother lived in Wyoming. The two of them must have left just before we got to the house and forgotten the map."

"We should immediately follow them. I have a feeling that Eduardo and I can do that alone without Nano. It will be less conspicuous, don't you think?"

"No, I don't think. The two of you together are Three Stooges short of a Stooge. And the one you're short of is Shemp."

"I'm sorry, Don Cassagrande. I do not know these Stooges...?"

"Well, Eduardo, the Three Stooges were three fucking idiots. Shemp was the least fucking idiotic. So basically, what I'm saying is that the two of you are complete fucking morons, and so I'm going to tell you the plan." The Don used the word 'fucking' as if he were punching a heavy bag in a boxing gym.

Just as he was about to explain his plan, he was interrupted by a big head that suddenly appeared from behind the door to the living room. "Excuse me, boss," said the huge pock-marked face, which was attached to an equally large body.

"What is it, Sammy?" asked the don, who didn't seem to mind being interrupted.

"We just got a call."

"Yes...."

"From Mike O'Malley over at the *LA Times*."

"And...."

"Well, he got a call from a man who is with the belly dancer."

"And this man said?"

Clearly, thought Eduardo, Sammy, whoever he was, had a hard time stringing thoughts together. And yet the don was patient and smiled encouragingly at the enforcer.

"He sent a message."

"Go on, Sammy"

"Well, they want to give us the book back."

"Yes, yes...."

"And we have a number for the man's cellphone."

"And...." The slightest hint of frustration had crept into the don's voice.

"And nothing, that was it."

"Well," said Bobby, "If they want to give us the book back, then let's just call this guy and arrange it."

"I agree," Eduardo chimed in. "The sooner we get it back the better."

"It don't work like that." Don Casagrande stood up and walked over to the window, where he stared out at his prancing animal bushes.

"But it makes sense, Pop."

"It makes no sense, Bobby. What the fuck is wrong with you? How many times do I have to tell you what the hell we do? We are not in the business of making nice." He shook his hands in a limp-wristed fashion as if casting aspersions on his son's manhood.

"Why do you always do that?" Bobby asked looking hurt.

"Why do you always do that?" mocked the don. "I tell you why I do that. You and this Eduardo, this man dressed like an Indian pimp, are fucking everything up. Your uncle," this to Eduardo, "told me that as far as he is concerned, Nano can crack your head like a walnut."

Both Bobby and Eduardo started to protest.

"No, shut the fuck up," yelled the don. "You don't say nothing from now on. I'm gonna tell you what we are doing. And if you do it, you, Eduardo, may live. And Bobby, you may not be forced to become a priest. Understood? Good.

"Now, we have the map. We know where they are heading. We have the phone number and we have our contacts in the Los Angeles police department tracking the phone with this new technology they have. So the two of you are going to follow them and you will be with Nano and Sammy. And when you find them, Nano and Sammy will soften them up until they give you their book or tell you where it is. Nano and Sammy will then kill them. Then," he paused, "the two of you will cut off their heads with a hacksaw, and you will bring them back here. You have ten minutes to pack your clothes and then meet Nano and Sammy in the front." With that the don stormed out the room and was soon in his garden chopping the heads off a troop of bushy baboons.

"God," groaned Bobby. "I hate that fucker. I hate the way he belittles me and I curse the day I was born into this family."

"Well, at least you're not going to be killed by a dwarf. My uncle is a disgusting man. Everything for him is about pain and killing. There is no negotiation. Anyway, what are we going to do? I don't think I could cut off anybody's head and I certainly don't want my own head squashed by Nano."

"Yeah, well, me neither, and I am certainly not going to become a priest. And I know my father, that's just his way of saying he's going to get rid of me."

"No, you're wrong, Bobby. No father would have his own son killed. My uncle, on the other hand, would love me to be dead."

"I wish I was wrong, Eduardo. I suspect my father tried to kill me a number of times during the course of my life. Or at least he would have killed me if my mother hadn't stopped him. Do you know how many times she had to take away the loaded gun he let me play with? Now she's been dead for a year, so this is his big chance. It seems we really are skewered like two kebabs over the same bed of hot coals."

Bobby squeezed Eduardo's shoulder. "We have no choice at this stage. Let's get our stuff and meet those two goons outside. And then there's a long way to go. Things can change on the road."

Bobby walked back to his room and took out a small overnight bag. He opened his wardrobe and looked at the perfectly hung white linen suits and pale blue shirts. He started to take a suit off the hanger and stopped. He obviously wouldn't need a suit for the trip. The question was, would he need anything? Thinking back to his mother, he felt a great sadness. It was she who'd wanted him to become a priest, not his father.

And now he knew why. She'd known he was not cut out to be a gangster. And she'd been absolutely right. The whole idea of whacking people and being splattered with blood wasn't something he had any interest in. The problem was the priesthood was of no interest to him either. What very few people knew about Bobby Casagrande was that he was still a virgin, and a conflicted one at that. All he wanted was to find someone to love, someone who'd love him in return. At this point he was ambivalent as to who or what that might be.

Bobby decided he would have taken a gun if he had one, but he didn't. The only weapon he possessed was a switchblade he'd bought in Naples. He flicked it open and felt the blade. It was only three inches long and rather dull and wouldn't have done anything more than rip a hole in Sammy's jacket. So he put it away, resigned to whatever fate had install for him. It didn't matter: he didn't really have that much to live for at this point.

Ten minutes later, with Nano wearing his porkpie hat, Sammy in the driver's seat, and Eduardo and Bobby in the way back, the big GMC Suburban made its way out of the Casagrande compound and turned towards Worland, Wyoming.

Nano's huge bag was in the middle row. Eduardo still had no idea what was in it.

# CHAPTER 18

The road to Worland.
*If you ask for nothing, you're sure to get it.*

Charley was all for hitting the major highways for as far as possible to try to get to Worland quickly. But Fanny had other ideas. "If they've got the map, then they'll know exactly how we're going to get there. I think we should take back roads."

"The problem is no matter which way we go, they can track us through my cell phone."

"Not if you take the battery out. They can't track us then. We'll just use pay phones and your cell phone in an emergency. If they pick up that signal, and we're on the back roads, it'll take them longer to intercept us."

Charley looked at her in amazement. "How do you know all these things, Fanny? I mean you seem to know something about everything. Codices, GPS tracking technology...."

"I read a lot, Charley. You look surprised...."

"I am, I don't know a lot of people who know anything about such diverse subjects."

"Well, at least you didn't say 'woman.' That would have said something about you I didn't want to imagine."

"Good God, no. Not me. Never would have said that. Nope, never. Not in a million years."

"Well, I'm glad to hear that," said Fanny, who didn't believe a word. "I despise men who think that way."

"Well, don't despise in my direction," laughed Charley nervously, making a firm commitment never to think that way about women again. "Now, what we do need to worry about is if they're ahead of us and get to your mom's house first. We don't want to put her in any danger. Maybe you should call and warn her."

"Don't worry about my momma. She's like Paula. Knows how to handle strange men."

"You mean she's a dominatrix?"

"Don't be ridiculous. She owns the place. She doesn't do that stuff anymore."

Charley was trying to process this information. "So you're saying your mom was a dominatrix...?"

"No, she was never into that sort of thing. Just a simple country whore who did normal stuff. You know what I mean?"

"Well, I'm not sure...." The thought of Fanny describing subjects of a sexual nature was extremely appealing. Then he thought better of it. "Actually, I do know what you mean ... I mean, not what your mom does obviously. You said she owns the place?"

Fanny looked at him with a puzzled expression on her face. Then she laughed. "Relax, Charley. I can't imagine how strange it must be to hear about someone who didn't grow up in middle-America with normal parents. But I didn't, and that's just how it is. You can ask me anything you like. My mom owns a brothel, a really beautiful old farm house right on the Big Horn River. She has twenty whores and they're kept pretty busy by the cattlemen and oil guys. She also has five big guards who take care of any trouble. That's why I'm not that worried."

For someone who was used to the world's most brutal warlords and mercenaries telling him what they did for a living, Charley had to admit he was astounded. Fanny was talking as if everything her mom did was normal. And yet far from turning Charley off, the nonchalant way that Fanny talked made her even more appealing. He only hoped that Fanny hadn't been one of her mom's employees, and in this regard Fanny seemed to have read his mind.

"I don't want you to think that what my mom does is something I aspire towards, Charley. I understand it and I most certainly don't think any less of her for carrying on the family business. But she's the one who wanted something different for me. Three generations of whoring was as much as she wanted in her life."

"Three generations?" The story was becoming even more intriguing by the minute.

"Oh, yes: my great-grandma owned a whorehouse in Texas, and my grandma owned it after her. Until those men burnt it down and killed my grandma. But I'll tell you that tonight over dinner when we stop. And we should think about that pretty soon. It's going to get dark and these roads aren't the best place to be after dark."

As much as Charley wanted to hear the story then and there, Fanny seemed to have shut down, and she remained that way until half an hour later when they pulled into the Nugget Hotel and Gambling Hall in Pahrump, Nevada.

Fanny and Charley were sixty miles west of Las Vegas where, unbeknownst to them, a big black GMC Suburban was cruising Fremont, carrying two men who wished they'd never heard of Fanny and her companion, and two who wanted to hurt them rather badly.

The question of two rooms didn't come up when Fanny and Charley registered at the front desk. As he had done back at the Sunset Hermitage, Charley began to project what would happen that night. But this time was different. While pure lust and longing were still evident in the slight sheen that covered his face, and in the palpitations of his heart, which seemed to him to be deafening, the desire to kiss her and hold her was stronger than his need to ravage her. Once again, Fanny came to his rescue.

"I know what you're thinking, Charley," she said with her curiously wry smile.

"What? What am I thinking?"

"You're thinking that you want to jump into bed with me and make love?"

"Well, that's um, true but...."

"And I want to make love to you, too. I honestly do. But I don't want to just have sex with you. And you are the only man I've ever met that I've said that to, because I like you a lot. More than a lot, in fact."

Charley held his breath

"I've thought about it," Fanny said, heaving her duffle onto the bed. "It's true I don't know enough about you yet, but the feeling I have is different from any feeling I've ever had. I'm not sure exactly what it is. Maybe it's love, we'll see." She unzipped her duffle and took out one of the dresses she'd bought at Walmart.

"Well, I love you, Fanny. I'm convinced of that. And I don't know half the things about you that I want to know. But I am absolutely sure."

"Good." She walked round the bed and kissed him on the cheek, causing him to once again briefly lose his mind. "But we aren't going to make love today."

Charley's face fell.

"We're going to wait until we're safe. When there's no one chasing after us. I want our first time to be perfect."

"But what happens if they do catch us, then we'll never get the chance. And we'll be missing out on something special." A note of desperation had crept into his voice.

"Then you, my darling, had better make sure they don't catch us. Now come," she said as she pulled him up off the bed. "Let's go eat dinner."

The Stockman's Steakhouse at the hotel was just the sort of place where two people who didn't want to be seen wouldn't be seen. Unless of course one of the people happened to be Fanny. The atmosphere was dark and clubby, and the portions at other tables looked large enough to demand, under normal circumstances, the full attention of the diners. But most of the men and a number of women looked up as Fanny walked by. The dress she'd bought at Walmart wasn't anything as fancy as the ones Alexander had worn when she and Charley went out to nice restaurants. But on Fanny it was stunning. It was a warm burgundy color with a ruffled front and it came down to just above her knees. Her knees, however, were not what was attracting attention, and when the maître d' shamelessly peered at her décolletage, Charley steered her into a booth at the back and gave the obsequious man a threatening glare.

"Would you like wine, Fanny?" he asked as they opened their menus, realizing that other than the Subway sandwiches they picked up in Victorville, they'd never eaten a meal together.

"I'm not really a wine drinker, Charley. But you know what I would like? A big, really dry gin martini."

"Wow, I never took you for a martini girl."

"What did you take me for ... a Shirley Temple girl?"

"No, no." He held his hands up in defense, realizing that once again he'd sounded arrogant. "I just meant ... I have no idea what I meant. I guess we really don't know anything about each other. I have no idea what you drink. So let me start again. Fanny, what would you like to drink?"

"It's okay, Charley. We agreed we don't know anything about each other yet. Except for your stories about Bosnia and other war-torn places, I have no idea about your background, or your life, or what you like and don't like.

"And you have about the same amount of information about me. But I've been with enough men...," she laughed as his face fell, "... not in that way. I mean I've had enough experience with men to know that you're special. I can tell you're kind and you're nice, and I just know what you feel for me is genuine, because it's what I feel for you. And I don't think those are the sort of feelings you can lie about without being caught out. I'd see it in your face and you'd see it in mine. Or maybe you wouldn't because men don't pick those things up as easily as women. I also know you won't take advantage of me and that you'll take care of me. Maybe they're just feelings, but I learned to trust my feelings a long time ago. And all of that is far more important than anything else. But let's order and then you can tell me something about your background and I'll tell you the story of mine."

After ordering martinis that came in glasses the size of goldfish bowls, Charley endeavored to do just that.

"I saw some horrible things in the Congo that I still have nightmares about. But there's one thing where this mercenary, a Belgian...."

Fanny put her fingers on his lips, stopping him in mid-exaggeration. "Charley, stop. Those aren't really the things I want to know about you. I want to know where you grew up. I want to know about your parents. What you were like when you were a little boy...."

"Oh, okay, but I think all of that would bore you. I had a very uneventful childhood."

"That's the problem with most men. You think impressing women with all of the 'manly' things you've done is going to make you sexier. If we're going to be together, then we really have to know each other, and your days as someone who covered war and violence don't tell me that much."

"Well, that's not what I was...."

"Yes, it was. Now listen to me, Charley. I already know you're smart and I've seen how brave you are when we were running from those hoodlums in the restaurant. You're funny and you're interesting, and we both said we feel something about each other that we haven't felt for anyone else. You called it love and I haven't called it anything yet. But I want to know what it is, and I think the only way I can find that out is if we talk about stuff that really says who we are. So now, try. Start at the beginning and let me decide what's important and what's not."

Charley took her hand and stared into her eyes. He'd marveled at her face before, and he'd looked into her eyes, but he'd never really examined them the way he had the rest of her body. They were a deep, brilliant green. More emerald than jade, with tiny flecks of blue and brown. They were laughing eyes more than crying eyes, he decided. The kind that pulled things out of you rather than pulling you in.

"Okay, but don't say I didn't warn you. It's not a pretty story."

"Let me be the judge of that," she replied.

"I grew up in Connecticut. My dad was a banker and my mom a preschool teacher...."

"Are they retired?"

"No, they were both killed in a car accident when I was in college."

"Jesus! How can you say you had an uneventful childhood? Having your parents killed in a car accident is horrible. I'm so sorry, Charley."

"Well, you're right. Not uneventful, exactly. Anyway, it got weird from that moment on."

"What do you mean?"

"Well, the ironic part about the accident was that they were driving back from the office of a divorce lawyer. They actually hated each other."

"I bet that messed with your brain a bit."

"I suppose it did, in a way, but I'm not sure how exactly. Probably made me worry less about dying than I did about trying to stay alive. That's most likely why I volunteered for some dangerous assignments. But I know I do exaggerate them a lot." He smiled at her.

"And how about now? Are you still not worried about staying alive?

"Of course, I am. Do you think I want to lose you now? Fanny, I want to be with you forever."

"Forever's a long time. Plus it's a slightly big ask for two people who just met." Fanny knew she was touching a nerve, but she needed him to slow down and the only way to do that was to get him to truly open up.

"I know, but it's what I want. Which is a heck of a lot different than how I felt two days ago."

"Well, I'm glad to hear that. But that's exactly why you need to talk. Now, tell me more about your 'embarrassing' childhood. And then I'll tell you mine, and we can decide whose was worse."

"All right, I can't wait to see how you'll top mine. So, as cavalier as this sounds, the only good thing that came out of my parent's death is that they left me a lot of money."

"Well, here's the first thing you should know about me: I don't care that you have a lot of money. That's not what I want to know about you. That sounds like you're trying to impress me again."

"No, no, no. I'm sorry, Fanny. I screwed that up., I just haven't thought about it for a long time. Money isn't the most important thing. And I know that sounded flippant. I honestly didn't mean it that way."

"I's okay, Charley." She squeezed his hand and a jolt surged up his arm, almost frazzling his brain. "But you must have cared about your parents."

"That's really my point. I thought I did, but it turns out we were living two very distinct lives. It was the money that made me understand what kind of people my parents were."

He'd been in his one-bedroom apartment when he got the call nineteen years before, writing an investigative paper for his graduate class on why mustaches have played such a big part in Slavic totalitarian regimes. It was not the initial shock that nearly put him over the edge, but rather the cumulative effect of the subsequent revelations that began the next day when he flew back to Connecticut. The house, though large, was literally bursting at the seams with what he thought were relatives and friends come to pay their respects and offer their prayers and condolences. Charley hadn't known or recognized half of them until his uncle took him aside to explain.

"To explain what?" asked Fanny when Charley said this.

"That most of the people in the house weren't actually relatives or even close friends for that matter. They were my parents' sexual partners."

"Well, with my background, I should understand. But I'm not sure I do. What are you saying? That your parents ran a brothel like my mom? Or that they slept around a lot?"

"More of the latter. My parents belonged to the largest swinger's club in Greenwich. Hell, they founded and owned the damn thing. God knows what subject my mom taught preschoolers. Unless of course they start sex education really early in Connecticut. According to some of the people, and these were incredibly successful lawyers, bankers, CEOs, my mom was the top performer for three years in a row. I've never quite got the picture of what she must have done to be so highly rated out my mind."

"That's terrible," said Fanny with what sounded like genuine sympathy. "I mean that sort of thing shouldn't shock me, but at least I knew what my mom was from the word go. Or shortly after the word go."

"Maybe you should tell me more about your childhood. It might make me feel better in telling you about mine."

"No, I want you to finish. It feels like you're getting rid of things, and I want you to do that till there isn't any mystery left."

Charley nodded and took a sip of his martini. Talking to Fanny was cathartic, and he knew in his heart that he'd have to get to *Porky Asses* at some point, but he wasn't sure he was ready. She was slowly drawing the guilt and shame out of him, and the more he talked to her the more he realized exactly why he'd never been able to tell anyone else about that night.

"Don't be sad, Charley. I'm not going to judge you."

"I know. But you have to know I've never told anyone else about this."

"Not even your ex-fiancée?"

"God, no. Especially not Alexandra. Talk about judging someone ... she would have told every one of her friends and taken great pleasure in embarrassing me. She would have thought it really funny and added to my eccentric character. It would have been horrible."

"Well then, you're lucky that relationship is over."

"Yes, I am." He wanted to tell Fanny how good it felt to open up to her but decided he'd wait.

"Good, but I want to know what happened next."

"Well, I walked around like a zombie. People kept coming up to me to tell me how amazing my parents were. And like I said, they weren't talking about what nice, kind people they were. You seriously wouldn't believe how many men and even women raved about my mother's performance in the bedroom. I guess my dad just ran the club because his activities never came up. Anyway, the more they talked, the more I felt like throwing up. I finally did when some old blond who didn't look as if she had many original parts left on either her face or body came up and asked me to have sex with her. She was, as I found out, the chief of staff for the club, and her job was to make sure prospective members qualified. She said she'd give me a pass for a few day if I wasn't up to it just then. She also told me that the club members were keen to resume activities, and as the house ... now my house ... was where the debauchery took place, they needed my permission and participation. After I vomited all over her, I ran up to my room, where I smoked enough weed to supply a small commune and lay on my bed until I started wondering how many of the members had pounded the life out of the bedsprings while I was away.

"I came out for the funeral two days later and had a meeting with my parents' attorney to discuss my inheritance. The club must have been incredibly profitable because they left me a ton of money. I gave half of it away to various charities, lent some to a guy in California who now owns one of the world's biggest computer companies, and put the rest into stocks and bonds. I seriously wanted to burn the house down, but my lawyer suggested I sell it to the other club members. I did and promised myself I wouldn't touch the money. And I haven't, except to buy my apartment in New York."

Fanny took a sip of her martini and swirled it round her mouth as if she were coming up with the solution to Fermat's last theorem rather than a decision on whether she finally understood the man in front of her. She had no doubt that she could trust him. She felt a deep emotional attraction that she'd quietly decided could only be love because it was softer and warmer and crunchier than anything she'd felt for anyone else. But there was still something he wasn't telling her, just like the one thing she didn't want to tell him.

The uneasiness was broken by the arrival of their appetizers: crab-stuffed mushrooms for Fanny, and jalapeño mac and cheese bites for Charley. In between bites and large sips of their martinis, Charley filled Fanny in on his breakup with Alexandra. When they'd finished with their steaks and were sipping on a second martini, Fanny told her story.

# CHAPTER 19

Big Lake Texas and Worland Wyoming, twenty-four years before.
*You can't see the stars if you never look up.*

Packer's Lone Star Bar and All-Star Whorehouse was situated a few miles from Big Lake on the edge of the dry lakebed that gave the town its name. Its current owner was Abigail Packer, the second generation of Packer women whose fathers and lovers had all been oil and cattle men coming in to spend their hard-earned dollars on some of the finest whores in Texas. The Packers had never taken husbands. They needed men for money and progeny, but they didn't trust them one iota when it came to long-term relationships.

The one exception, Flo Packer confessed to her mom as they sat sipping bourbon on the porch after a particularly busy day, was the father of her daughter, Fanny. He was neither an oilman nor a cattleman. He could have been a vacuum cleaner salesman, like the ones who sometimes dropped by from Odessa or Midland and usually made jokes about "sucking

and blowing," but Flo doubted it. He was just too sophisticated to be anything as mundane as a traveling salesman. He had an accent that wasn't Texan or
American as far as anyone could tell, and he wasn't
Mexican. He had a wild mane of red hair and he was
far bigger than any of the prison guards who served as security to earn extra cash and blowjobs on
their days off from the nearby prison. The sex had
been so extraordinary, and so different to anything
Flo had experienced before, that she'd actually refused her usual $200 fee, and offered to pay him for
another round. He'd laughed and told her that she
was the perfect vessel for his seed and to take care
of their daughter because she would be special. The
red-haired man never explained how he knew Flo
would produce a daughter nor why she'd be special.
He simply patted her ample rump and disappeared
into the night.

Nine months later Flo gave birth to the most beautiful baby any of the whores had ever seen. She weighed a healthy nine pounds and exited Flo's womb
with a full head of bright red curly hair. The only person who had her suspicions of the dimpled little baby was Abigail. "You trust me, Flo, that little one's the
devil's spawn. No one in our family has ever had the
red hair. She's gonna bring us nuthin' but trouble."
Then she spat three time into the nearest spittoon
and drew a five-pointed hex sign over her heart.

Flo thought her mother was a crazy old coot, and
she doted on Fanny, who seemed to bring a smile to
the face of everyone she came into contact with in
the bordello. When Flo was busy, which she invaria-

bly was, Fanny was looked after by a retired whore that everyone referred to as Nona.

"Come, little one," called Nona as the now chubby five-year-old slipped on her nightdress. "Come listen to the crickets and watch the stars while I brush your hair."

The little girl scampered over and climbed onto the lap of the old woman who sat by the window. It was warm and comfortable snuggled into Nona's soft folds, and she looked out into the purple sky through little-girl eyes, and a strange peace came over her.

"See your hair," said Nona pointing to Fanny's reflection in the window. "It is as red as the tail of the comet that shoots through the sky."

"What's a comet, Nona?" asked Fanny.

"A comet is a star without a home, racing through the heavens, seeking a place to settle down."

"A place like this, like our house?"

"No," laughed the old woman. "Not like this house."

"Like what then? What's wrong with our house?"

"I don't know, child. That's something to ask your mother."

"But Momma never has time to talk to me. She's always busy. What does she do, Nona?"

"You ask too many questions sometimes. Hush a while and I'll tell you a story."

"But I don't want to hush, Nona. I want to know what Momma does all the time with the men who come in to her special room. I want to see the special room." Fanny crossed her little arms and stuck out her lower lip.

"You stop immediately, young lady. Why are you spying on your momma like that?"

Fanny was smart enough to know that an angry Nona was not a good thing to be around, and so she threw her arms round the old lady's neck and buried her head in Nona's saggy breasts. "I'm sorry, Nona, please don't be angry with me?"

"Oh, child. I'm not angry with you. Your momma loves you very much, but she has work to do with those men. It's nothing to concern yourself with. Just stay away from them. They're not good."

Suddenly the song of the crickets ended, replaced by the shrill whine of badly tuned engines. Three pickup trucks had pulled up outside the front of the house. Men got out. Men with guns. And then the men began to shout. Fanny didn't understand what they were saying, but she heard them calling for her grandma and momma. She heard them getting angrier and angrier and they waved their guns at her grandma, who came out onto the front porch. Then Nona pushed her aside and stuck her head out the window. She screamed at the men to go away and leave them alone.

One minute Nona had her head out the window and the next there was a loud bang as a comet floated up from the ground and found a home right where Nona's head used to be.

Fanny didn't remember much of anything else. Just the screaming and the crying as her momma rushed into the room and grabbed her and carried her out of the house as the flames turned the Texas sky the color of her hair.

"Christ, Fanny. That's horrific. I'm so sorry you had to go through that." He squeezed her hand and she smiled sadly. "Who were those guys?"

"I was so little and my momma never talked about it much, but there was a big new-age Baptist church nearby and I suppose they were religious nuts doing what they thought was God's work. After we buried Nona and my grandma, who died right there on the porch that night, Momma bought a big-old second-hand bus and she drove us and ten of the whores who hadn't lost their nerves north. I remember we stopped a lot along the way outside small towns."

"And the bus was like a traveling brothel?"

"I suppose in a way. Obviously, I was too young to understand then, but I know now that the bus was an old Bookmobile. Except the men took out whores the way other people used to take out books. They still have it by the way."

"That's a story in itself. Do you know how it worked?" The journalist in Charley had wormed its way to the surface through the potholes and pitfalls of his infatuation.

"Not everything, because I never really wanted to know. But as I understand it, my mom stocked it with all sorts of erotic literature and set it up using the Dewey Decimal System. So a man would come in and browse the shelves and decide on what sort of thing he wanted, and then my mom would delegate the appropriate whore for the job. There were two bedrooms at the back of the bus. Now that's all I know, and I'm a little embarrassed to discuss it further. I know it's an interesting story, but it's a sad one.

"It is. But the best stories usually are."

"I don't know. I like happy stories. Anyway, after six months the bus finally broke down in Worland. By then Momma had made enough money to start again. And that's where I grew up and went to school."

"But how did you become a belly dancer?

Fanny sighed and hooked an olive from her nearly empty glass. "I told you I didn't want to get into the family business and my momma didn't want me to either. But when you've lived that kind of life, there aren't that many things that look interesting. Or maybe there are and I just wasn't motivated. The good news about the Bookmobile is that we ended up with a big library. It was stocked, mainly with erotic books, but there were sets of encyclopedias and other literature that I could read. And I read them all. The ones I read the most were the books on Greek and Roman mythology. Something about the ancient gods and goddesses always fascinated me."

But Charley, who was hovering somewhere between empathy and horniness, was fascinated by something else entirely. "Did you read the erotic stuff?"

"You'll just have to wait to find out." Fanny laughed.

"I'm not sure I can."

"Well, you're going to have to. Don't interrupt. There was only one thing I used to dream about constantly, and that was finding out who my father was. For some reason, even though I thought it was probably going to be impossible, I wanted to meet him. And I knew I'd never do that from the reception desk, where I worked, at a whorehouse in Wyoming."

"Hang on, Fanny. And I know I'm interrupting again but please, before you tell me more, explain to me why you say whores and whorehouse? Those terms sound quite derogatory."

"They are when you say them. But for those of us in the business—and you know I'm really not in the business, but I grew up in it—whore is a perfectly acceptable term. You should probably say sex-worker or prostitute."

"Okay, sorry. Got it. I didn't want to be offensive. So in all the time growing up, you had no idea who your father was?"

"No, and neither did my mother. All she ever told me was that he was a big handsome man with wild red hair who talked with a strange accent. But none of the other women knew him, and he never came back. I had this vision of him. That he was someone famous. Maybe a secret agent, or a Hollywood actor in disguise."

"I guess that's perfectly understandable. A lot of kids fantasize about their parents being something special. The truth, however, is mostly a let-down. Especially in my case. I'm not sure anyone wants to know their mother is a star sex performer."

"Well, mine was and I was okay with that."

"Touché. Anyway, where does belly dancing fit into this...?"

"So when I was growing up, we had movie night every Sunday after dinner. Regular movies, not porn or anything. And every male movie star I saw I imagined was my dad. Then one Sunday we saw this movie called *Son of Sinbad* with Sally Forrest, who does this incredible dance at the end of the movie. I knew that night it was what I wanted to do. I loved dancing and it seemed like I was designed for belly dancing. And the best belly dancing school, as I found out, was in Los Angeles."

"So you could look for your dad at the same time?"

"Exactly, but it didn't take long to realize what a stupid and pointless dream that was."

"Why did you feel that way?"

"Because obsession blinds you to the facts."

"Maybe you're right. But I think sometimes you just have to throw yourself into the pursuit of a dream. Even if it seems totally hopeless."

"Well I threw myself into dancing instead." Fanny seemed slightly annoyed at Charley's inadvertent condescension. "Anyway, to finish my story, I did really well. I danced at events and a few restaurants, and then I was asked to perform in a segment on various forms of dancing on *Good Morning America*. I guess that's where Eduardo's people saw me. And suddenly, now I'm really tired, Charley."

"Of course, Fanny. It's been a long day."

"It has, but I don't mean sleepy. I guess I'm just really tired of my life so far. I'm tired of the searching and the pretending and the running. I've done some things I wish I hadn't. Nothing criminal, in case you're wondering, just things I wouldn't normally do, but I did because I needed the money."

"Fanny," said Charley, moving over to her side of the booth and putting his arm around her, "I don't know what's going to happen over the next few days. I don't know what you did for money and I don't care. All I know is that I am so in love with you and I cannot imagine life without you and I am going to do everything I can to protect you...."

"Oh, Charley...," she interrupted.

"No, let me finish. I realize we've only known each other for a few days but in my whole life I've never felt so ... and I don't even know what the right word is ... infatuated, maybe."

It was Fanny's turn to shush him, and she did it with a kiss. It was her seventh kiss, but it was a kiss unlike any that Charley could possibly have imagined. He'd never had religion. Never believed in a higher power, or angels, or any beings of that ilk. But Charley got religion from that kiss. It might, he thought before his brain exploded, be the two martinis that had put him on top of the heart-wrenching rollercoaster. But it was her lips that pulled him into the black hole in which stars begin and gods are born. Then, as her velvet tongue glided between his teeth and touched his, he felt himself float above the table, far above the man and woman below, locked in each other's arms. And Fanny was with him, and he saw her perhaps for the first time for what she was.

Then, as suddenly as it had begun, it was over, and they were back in the booth. She wanted to go to sleep with him next to her in bed, but not in her. That would have to wait.

# CHAPTER 20

Las Vegas, the same night.
*Bad plans, like hard-boiled eggs, don't hatch.*

"It's nearly 8:30," said Bobby. "We're not going to find them tonight, Sammy. I don't know about the rest of you, but I'm starving." They'd been cruising Las Vegas for four hours trying to catch a glimpse of Fanny and Charley. Sammy looked over at Nano, who nodded his head in what Eduardo assumed was consent.

"Okay," Sammy replied.

"Okay, what?" Bobby asked.

"Okay, we stop for the night."

"Oh, thank God," said Eduardo. "My coglioni have blisters on them the size of ravioli."

"That's exactly what I feel like," Bobby said, getting quite excited and forgetting for a moment that he was possibly talking about his and Eduardo's last meal. "Cheese ravioli with meatballs. Sammy, let's go to Chicago Joe's? I know you and my dad love that place. Eduardo, it's real old-school Las Vegas Italian. You're going to love it."

Eduardo, who really was old-school Italian, doubted that. Nano, however, who hadn't grunted much since they'd left Los Angeles, got quite animated at the mention of Chicago Joe's.

"Okay, Nano," Sammy said, "you got it, my friend."

"What's he want?" asked Eduardo, who'd by now given up trying to understand the dwarf.

"He agrees."

"That's great. So long as Nano's happy," said Bobby with more than a hint of sarcasm. "Well, let's stop talking so much and go."

"Nano says he wants the pasta with snails, and plenty of it. His favorite. Me and him and your dad, we used to go to Chicago Joe's a lot in the old days." This was Sammy's longest sentence to date. "We eat, then we check in to the Stardust. Your dad, he organized rooms."

There was a line to get in to Chicago Joe's, but Sammy and Nano ignored it and simply walked in. The owner rushed up to Sammy and made a big show of embracing him. He gave Bobby a hug and nodded at Eduardo, who put out his hand but was ignored. Eduardo didn't mind: it looked like some low-class establishment in any case. Like a little old house in which the owners seemed to have forgotten to take down their Christmas lights.

A few people gawked as they made their way over to a table at the back, and more than a number of the guests seemed to know Sammy and the dwarf. They sat down, and the owner came over with two bottles of Chianti Classico. He poured Sammy, Bobby, and Eduardo each a glass and gave Nano the other bottle, which the dwarf half-emptied in one gulp.

"My God," Eduardo said after he'd taken a sip. "I hope the food is better than the wine."

"Relax, Eduardo," Bobby said. "They will bring us stuff you're going tell people about back in Rome, trust me."

Eduardo doubted it, but he was distracted by Nano, who had picked up a bread roll and squashed it into a ball the size of an apricot. He popped it in his mouth and grinned at Eduardo as if giving a demonstration of precisely what he had planned for Eduardo's head.

A moment of tense silence ensued, and then Sammy cleared his throat. "Hey, Bobby," he said, holding his massive hand up as if to encourage a little patience. "You know Eduardo is not going to get back to Rome. Nano is going to kill him."

"What do you mean? My father said everything would be fine if we got the book back and killed the fat chick and the guy."

"I told you she's not fat, she's large...."

"Shut up, Eduardo. Didn't you hear what Sammy just said? Nano is going to kill you anyway. Even if we get the book back."

Nano snarled at Eduardo and crushed another bread roll between his hairy hands.

"I probably said too much," Sammy mumbled.

"Well, that's a fucking change for you," Eduardo said. "This is crazy. What the hell is wrong with you people?"

"I'm going to call my dad. There's obviously been some miscommunication." Although of course Bobby knew there wasn't, he didn't want to give Sammy the impression that he already knew. He and Eduardo needed all the time they could get to hatch a plan.

"I'm sorry, Bobby." Sammy patted him on the shoulder in a demented though avuncular sort of way. "You know I like you a lot."

"You have a fantastic way of showing it."

"I've known you since you were a baby."

"For fuck's sake, Sammy. Please, just speak in full thoughts for once. What the hell are you supposed to do?"

"Our orders, Nano's and mine, are to get the book, kill the big woman and her man, and then ... kill both of you."

"What the fuck, Sammy. My dad said he was going to have me become a priest, not kill me."

"Yeah, well, it would embarrass him to see you in church. And he knows you'd hate it. It's a kindness."

"Oh, forgive me. A painful death is a kindness? Well, for your information I'd hate becoming a priest a lot less than being fucking killed. Jesus, Sammy."

"Calm down, Bobby. And don't worry, I'll make it quick. You won't feel a thing. I don't think Nano will do the same for this Italian finocchio, though. His uncle kind of hates him."

Eduardo snorted at this. "You're all pazzo. You call a woman who would have been worshipped by Titian fat, and you call me, a man of unquestionable heterosexual tastes, gay. You sicken me." He spat on the floor, much to the horror of a blond woman at the next table.

"Eduardo, for God's sake. Didn't you just hear what they said? They're going to kill us, no matter what happens."

Eduardo, as slow-witted as he may have been, knew what Bobby was trying to do, and so, channeling his inner thespian, played along. "Yes, I heard that, my friend. But I can't imagine it to be true. My uncle is a terrible person for sure, but his bark, as you Americans say, is worse than his teeth. He is always threatening me and hitting me at times, it's true, but he would not kill me. I am the last of the Sabatinis. We go back hundreds, possibly thousands of years." He picked up the remaining bread roll, squeezing it gently into a ball, and tossed it at Nano, who caught it in his mouth.

Bobby stared at Eduardo in disbelief. He knew his friend was terrified of the dwarf. But Eduardo smiled back and rolled his eyes in an odd way.

"I don't get it, Sammy. Why would you tell us this now ... at dinner ... at the beginning? Why wouldn't you just wait until we get the book back?"

"Your dad didn't say when to tell you, Bobby. So I figured I'd do it now and get it over with. Then it won't be such a big surprise and we can enjoy our meal. Your dad doesn't want you to be too upset. He still loves you."

"Fuck him being upset. I don't care how he feels. And how do you know he loves me? What are you, his confidant?"

Bobby could have sworn that Sammy's face, normally the hue of an overripe radish, became even more red.

"Well, I hope he fucking slips off the ladder while he's pruning his abominable animals and impales himself on his hedge trimmers."

"Don't talk badly about your dad. He's a good man. Show some respect."

"A good man? He makes Stalin look like a good man. At least Stalin didn't kill his own son."

"Although," said Eduardo, "I believe he tried once or twice."

At that moment, some men who were perhaps slightly smaller than Sammy, but clearly, from their questionable taste in clothes and gold chains, wiseguys, waved at them from a few tables over. Nano got all excited and tugged at Sammy's sleeve. Sammy stopped his admonition of Bobby and looked over.

"Hey, Nano, it's Rocky and Edo Bonnano."

Nano grunted something, and Sammy stood up.

"You're right. We have to go pay our respects. Come, you too, Bobby."

"No, fuck you and fuck the Bonnanos. I'm staying here." Bobby looked over at Eduardo, who rolled his eyes again.

"Suit yourself, Bobby, but your dad wouldn't be happy if he found out."

"Really? Well, why don't you call him right now and tell him exactly what I said. Maybe he'll ask you to slap me before you kill me."

Sammy shook his head and muttered something about young people. Then he and Nano walked over to the Bonnano table and began to talk. He must have mentioned the impending dispatch of Eduardo and Bobby, because the Bonannos looked over, laughed, and made lewd gestures.

"Do you believe this shit, Eduardo?"

"I believe it, my friend, and I have to say you would be an excellent actor too. Very natural gestures and laid-back projection."

"Thank you. Yes, it feels good, I must say. Your stagecraft is wonderful. Not a hint of nervousness. I think we managed to confuse them. But why do you keep rolling your eyes?"

"I am not calm," Eduardo whispered, his voice quivering. 'I am extremely frightened in here." He patted his chest. "But, like you, I don't want them to think that. And look, I'm not rolling my eyes, I am pointing with them to the car keys. That idiot has left them on the table. So come on, quickly, let's go." Eduardo made to get up, nearly pulling the tablecloth off.

'Wait, Eduardo."

"No time, Bobby. It's now or never."

'I'm with you, but we have to do this with a little subtlety. Those two thugs may be idiots, but they'll get us before we get away if we aren't careful." Bobby slid the keys off the table and put them in his pocket. "I'll take the keys, then I'll walk over to the bathroom and slip out the back. You can see the car from here. As soon as you see me in it, get up and walk to the door as quickly as you can. Got it?"

"Yes, I got it, but be careful. That little bastard Nano is quick."

"Well, you have to be quicker, Eduardo. It's our only chance." Bobby stood up, pretended to cramp, and hobbled over to a waiter, who pointed to the bathroom. Both Sammy and Nano looked over to see what was happening. Eduardo waved and pointed to his stomach and then at the back of his pants as if to say Bobby had had an accident. It must have worked, because Sammy just shook his head in disgust and went back to his conversation with Edo Bonnano. Nano, who was jabbering at Rocky, frowned suspiciously, and Eduardo felt his own guts rumble. The dwarf was not as easily fooled.

Eduardo glanced out the window and saw Bobby sneaking towards the car. His knees began to shake at the thought of what he was about to do. He looked back over at Nano and Sammy who didn't seem overly concerned by Bobby's lengthy trip to the toilet. At that moment, however, the waiter appeared with a huge tray of food destined for their table, and Eduardo made the decision that if he didn't move then, it would be too late. It very nearly was. Sammy and Nano saw the food and began to wrap up their conversation. So Eduardo stood up just as Sammy and Nano began to walk over.

"You know, I think Bobby must be really sick. I'd better go see before I eat. You will excuse me, please."

Sammy's arm shot out and his giant hand clamped on to Eduardo's wrist. "You don't go nowhere. Nano, you go look."

The dwarf nodded his assent and ambled towards the bathroom, grabbing a lamb chop off the blond woman's plate as he went by. Eduardo felt his heart begin to thump and sweat began to pour down his face.

"What's the matter?" Sammy asked. "You thinking of leaving us?"

Only then did he look down at the table to where he'd left the keys.

"You fucking rat bastard! The keys? Where are the keys?"

Eduardo, his panic escalating into the danger zone, didn't know what to do for a second. Then he took his cue from Sammy and screamed, "A rat! There's a rat!"

Pandemonium broke out. Men and women not connected to the mob assumed the word referred to a rodent rather than an informer, and started to shriek. Some even leapt on to their chairs. The Bonnano family members drew their guns and began to look around the room. The blond's companion, a swarthy individual with a pronounced sneer on his face, who hadn't reacted either to Eduardo spitting or Nano stealing the chop, suddenly pulled a sawed-off shotgun from under his large jacket and fired at the Bonannos. The shot went wild, missing them entirely but shattering windows and lights. The Bonnanos fired back, and Rocky yelled, "It's 'No Balls' Boschetto, get that fuckin' rat bastard."

Sammy, who had been slightly slower on the uptake, turned their table over, pulled out his gun, and began firing randomly into the room. It wasn't exactly what Eduardo had planned, but it worked perfectly. Putting his head down and beseeching the Virgin Mother, he sprinted over to the door, leapt down the stairs, and jumped into the front passenger seat just as Bobby gunned the engine. At that moment, Nano, who'd heard the commotion from the bathroom, burst out the front door and flung himself onto the hood of the SUV. He began to thump on the windshield and scream. Both Bobby and Eduardo screamed back in unison at the horrific apparition that clung precariously to the hood. Nano's face was twisted in pure hatred, and as he punched the windshield again, a large crack appeared. Bobby swung the wheel and the SUV spun across the street, grazing a parked Cadillac and dislodging Nano, who flew into a crowd of gawkers. The last Bobby saw of him was his enraged face with its porkpie topping still in place, sticking out between the legs of a large woman in the now terrified crowd.

"So what's your plan, Eduardo?" asked Bobby as he slowed the SUV and turned onto Charleston Boulevard.

"That was it, I'm afraid."

"What, steal the keys and make a dash for the car?"

"Hey, look. I can't work out what has happened. And I'm really sorry that you're involved, Bobby, and that your father is a despicable stronzo. All I know is we're still alive and maybe, if we can get the book back and get it to my uncle, perhaps they will change their minds. The good news is we have a head start on Sammy and Nano, and we have the map." He picked up the now crumpled map from the console and did his best to smooth it out. "Without this, they can't know the route. So we just take it and try to get to Fanny and the man before they get to Worland."

"Well, it's as good as anything, I suppose, and I have nothing better. But if we're doing this together, then you have to tell me what makes that book so valuable."

"Okay, I'll tell you, but it's not a short story."

"It's not a short ride, so go ahead."

Over the course of the next day as they drove along Route 15, stopping in Mesquite and Provo and countless other towns along the way, desperate for a sight of the large redhead and her unknown partner, Eduardo told Bobby the strangest tale he'd ever heard. If Eduardo hadn't exuded the intense passion that seemed to come out in every twist of the story, Bobby wouldn't have believed him. But Eduardo did, and Bobby had no choice.

Eduardo, a tall gangly sixteen-year-old, deprived of anything resembling love, brutalized by his uncle when he visited the Arcieri palace on a weekly basis to sleep with Eduardo's governess, herself a beast of a woman who took every opportunity to chastise her charge emotionally and physically, was sitting on his bed looking at the ancient book that had come into his possession that morning.

Strangely enough, the book had been in the palace the entire time, hidden in a secret compartment in the big wooden desk in the library, its hiding place known only to Eduardo's lawyer.

"Eduardo," said the lawyer once he was satisfied that he and Eduardo were alone in the library, "it is time for me to reveal this part of your inheritance. But I must warn you, your uncle Bruno would kill you to know its hiding place." He walked over to the big desk and began to manipulate a gold object that Eduardo had never really taken much notice of before. There was a click and a small door popped open on the side of the desk, revealing a secret compartment. The lawyer reached in and drew out a small leather-bound book that looked extremely ancient. Eduardo, who'd hoped the inheritance would have been a bag of priceless gems or at the very least a jeweled dagger with which to stab his uncle, looked crestfallen.

"A book?' Is that all I get?"

"Well, not all, Eduardo. Your father also left you this palace, which is worth a considerable fortune, and enough money in a trust account to live ten lifetimes without working. But this book...," he handed it to Eduardo who looked at it with a certain disdain, "as I understand from your late father, is the most valuable of all. It is a sacred text that has been in your family for centuries and promises something miraculous. You are to study it, and on your eighteenth birthday you will receive instructions on how to apply what you have learned. In the meantime, you are to keep its hiding place and contents a secret. Especially from your uncle, who I'm afraid will kill you if he knows you have it."

"He doesn't know of its existence?" asked Eduardo, feeling even more afraid than he normally did at the mention of Uncle Bruno.

"He does. But he believes it will only come into your possession on your twenty-fourth birthday. Your father arranged it this way in the hope that by the time you could get your hands on it, it would be too late. The prophesy in the book would already have come true."

"I'd rather have a jeweled stiletto than a stupid book. That would be more effective against my uncle."

"Perhaps, but keep in mind that I do not know what the book will do for you. Your father was silent on that subject. All I know is that you need to be careful. When you read it, do it in here and make sure the door is locked. And now, my young friend, I will leave you to your book and your lonely life. Call if you need anything, but not too often." And with that the lawyer, having done his job, turned and walked out, leaving the sad young man even sadder than he'd been before.

"Well," Eduardo continued his story to Bobby, "I ignored my lawyer's advice and took the book to my room to study it. It was clearly a very ancient book, but surprisingly enough the pages were not brittle. They were soft and warm, almost as if they had life. Much to my horror, when I could get my eyes away from the illustrations, I realized that the book was written in ancient Greek, a subject I'd been forced to study on the strict instructions of my father, but at which I had failed rather miserably. I didn't get more than a few words in because the pictures had captured my attention fully. Very detailed, very intricate, and much to the astonishment of my young mind, extremely arousing."

"And why was that?" asked Bobby, perking up a little.

"Well, you must understand I'd never had any experience with anything vaguely erotic except for hearing the terrible grunts and moans of my uncle and my governess as they went at it like two drunken animals in her bedroom, which was next to mine. But here in front of me were pictures of people engaged in sex. And not, as I came to discover, the kind of sexual acts that the average couple could perform. It was one afternoon, as I sat on my bed, looking at the illustrations and, I am embarrassed to say, pleasuring myself when my governess burst in.

"'Mother of God,' she screamed, seeing me in my tumescent state. 'What the hell are you doing, you wretch?' As you can imagine, I was in deep shock."

"After what you've said about her, I can only imagine, and no doubt your horniness vanished?"

"No, that was the strange part. If anything, I became even more horny. Now realize that my only physical contact with this woman, who could be considered attractive only to a man of my uncle's sick tastes, had been at the receiving end of her hand as she beat me about the head for the slightest infraction of whatever rules she'd decided were in order for my upbringing. And yet the more she shouted and flailed at me, the more aroused I became, until she grabbed both the book and my poor penis. All I can think, Bobby, is that she must have been so drunk from the wine and so unsatisfied by my uncle's poor performance that she absolutely needed to rip her clothes off, and before I even knew what was happening, she had attempted to perform position twenty-seven with me."

"My god, what happened?"

"Let me just say we both released together. Me over the clean bedclothes, and she into the arms of her maker."

"She was dead?"

"Oh, yes. She was dead all right. At first I panicked and assumed I'd murdered her. I dragged her back into her bedroom and put her on the bed. Then I called one of the servants, who in turn called my uncle, who sent over one of his lieutenants. He, fortunately, took care of everything. And that is when Uncle Bruno really became obsessed with getting the book. I think he felt that perhaps it was he that had caused her death after their vigorous lovemaking. It certainly gained him a reputation amongst the men, but alas for him, not amongst the women.

"The courtesan Bella Castiglione, whom my uncle sent over on my seventeenth birthday to establish if I preferred women to men, as he suspected, told me all about my uncle. I shall spare you the details...."

"I'd appreciate that."

"Let's just say he wasn't up to much. In fact, he wasn't up to anything."

"And you managed to keep the book secret?"

"Yes, up until three months ago when I turned twenty-four. That is when his people started looking for women for me. Although of course, really for him. And that is how I met Fanny."

# CHAPTER 21

A diner in a small town on the way to Worland.
*The road less traveled is usually a bad road.*

Charley looked at his watch and saw that it was only 4:30. Sleep had been both elusive and painful curled up on the small couch, and his back ached as he
walked over to the window. It was still dark outside
with just a hint of dawn creeping up over the hori-
zon. He thought back to the previous evening when
they'd got back to the room. Fanny had used the
bathroom first, changing into the nightgown she'd
bought at Walmart. There was nothing sexual about
the garment itself, thought Charley, other than the
fact that she was in it. She saw that he was staring,
and smiled as she got into the bed.

"Why don't you go and wash up and then come and
get into bed with me."

But he couldn't. Not yet. He knew that if he lay next
to her he'd be unable to control himself, and while
Fanny appeared to be disappointed at first, he knew
she understood. The seventh kiss, the one at dinner,
had changed everything. It had been the climax that

pulled him back from the almost total insanity of the last few days. Fanny was no longer simply an object of his desire or temporarily perverted lust. She had become something else entirely.

"Be strong, Charley. Think of us as two objects being pulled towards a giant magnet. Worland is the magnet and something wonderful is going to happen when we get there tomorrow." And with that she blew him a kiss and turned off the bedside light.

Charley lay on the small couch and stared into the darkness. Love, or at least his understanding of love, seemed to redefine itself with every breath in every moment. He felt like butter melting on a large stack of pancakes. Like a star being sucked into a black hole.

He looked over at Fanny snoring gently as the sunlight slowly made its way into the room. She lay on her back covered in the sheet, with her hair spread out over the pillow like a halo painted by Kandinsky or Klimt. More beautiful than anything he'd ever seen and more enchanting than anything he could have imagined. She must have felt him staring because just then, when he thought his heart would break, she opened her eyes.

"Oh, Charley, I just had this wonderful dream."

"About us?"

"Of course, about us. That was the wonderful part. We were flying over some mountains like two eagles. Looking down on the world below. It was so beautiful, Charley."

He smiled. "Sounds incredible, and I can't imagine anything I'd like to do more. But right now, I think we should leave. We don't know where those guys are, but we can't take any chances." And so it was that after they'd showered separately and dressed—she in the bedroom and he in the bathroom—they walked down to the car and set off for Worland. They were still a good eight hours away, but Charley thought if they stuck to the main road for most of the way, they would make Worland by early evening.

"I still don't know why you didn't you sleep next to me, Charley. I really wanted you to. I knew I could trust you."

"I wanted to, Fanny. I really did. More than you can know. But I couldn't. Not until we're safe."

She brushed his cheek with her hand and he felt the now familiar tingle that happened each time they touched. She said nothing more and closed her eyes and appeared to drift off into sleep, though Charley suspected she was pretending. It was better that way. They had a lot to talk about, but this wasn't the time. She woke up once when Charley stopped for gas, but dozed off again the minute they hit the highway

Four hours later as they entered the town of Eureka, Utah, Fanny woke up. She smiled dreamily and then pinched her face in pain. "Oops, I have to pee really badly."

"Me too, and I'm hungry and a little tired. Let's find a diner and take a thirty-minute break. I don't think we should chance much more than that. It would be a lot easier if we knew where those guys were."

"Maybe you should call your friend Mike again. See if he's heard anything more. And I suppose I should call my mom and tell her what to expect."

The Miner's Diner wasn't hard to find in a town with less than a thousand residents. It was exactly the kind of place you'd expect in an old mining town. Crammed with pictures of miners and mines and various mementos of the old west. It also smelled deliciously of fried food.

"Sit where you'd like, folks," said the friendly waitress, handing them two menus, "and I'll be right over. Bathrooms are there in case you need them."

After they'd both relieved themselves, they settled into a red booth and glanced at the menu.

"Just what I feel like," said Charley. "A hamburger and fries and a root beer float. God, I'm hungry."

"That's exactly what I feel like too, but I should probably go for a salad. I haven't worked out at all."

"Well, I bet you all the stress of the past few days has burnt off any calories you may have put on." He stopped himself. "Not that I think you put any on."

"How would you know?"

"What do you mean?"

"Well, if you saw me for the first time two days ago, how would you know if I'd put on any weight?"

"I wouldn't know … I mean I don't know … how could I know?"

"You couldn't, unless you'd seen me before…?"

Charley realized his nostrils were flaring and his breathing had changed. "Impossible, I'd never seen you before that restaurant."

She looked into his eyes as if she knew he was lying. Then she burst out laughing. "I'm just kidding you. You know what, I just want to hug you and hold you. You are the sweetest guy I've ever met, and when we get to my mom's place and we can both breathe easier, that's exactly what I'm going to do."

Charley hoped he could wait. He also hoped they'd actually make it to Worland, and so grinned like an idiot and said, "I can't wait for that either, Fanny. But in the meantime, here...." He took out his cellphone and reinserted the battery. "Call your mom. But try to be quick and take the battery out as soon as you're done. I'm going to go to that phone booth on the corner and try my pal. And order me the hamburger and fries."

He glanced through the window at Fanny as he walked up to the phone booth. He could barely make her out from where he was, but it looked as if she were on the phone. He put in a few quarters and dialed the number of the LA Times. Once again he was in luck, and Mike picked up on the first ring.

"Mike, it's Charley. Sorry to bug you, but I wonder if you've heard any more."

"Jesus, Charley. Are you okay?"

"Yeah, we're fine but I have no idea where those mob guys are."

"I don't either, but there's definitely been a complication since we spoke yesterday. There may actually be some good news."

"What? Tell me...." Charley felt his heartrate accelerate.

"There's also some bad news."

"Shit, well tell me the good news...."

"Apparently, according to my source who sounded worried, Bobby Casagrande and Eduardo Sabatini have split from Sammy and Nano Mortale."

"Why's that to our advantage? I don't get it. It seems like now we have two separate parties after us instead of one."

"Maybe, but my guy says Sammy and Nano were given orders to take out Bobby and Eduardo. As I said before, their families don't think too much of them and they seem to have fucked this up big time. They're in the same position as you, Charley."

"Okay, I guess that's good news. What's the bad news?"

"Sammy and Nano are still after you, and you're probably still the priority. Get both of you, get the object, whatever it may be, and then whack the others. So whatever you have that they want, it must be pretty valuable."

"Thanks, Mike, I really appreciate this. All I know is that it's a book."

"Jesus, what kind of book is worth cutting your heads off for?"

"Cutting our heads off?"

"Oh, yeah. Didn't I mention that? Apparently, that's what they've been ordered to do."

If the reality of the situation wasn't clear to Charley before, it was crystal now. His stomach contracted and his throat went dry. "I'll call you if anything happens."

"Hopefully you'll still be able to...."

Charley hung up and put his head in his hands. He wasn't sure what to think. The good news may have been potentially good, but the bad news was definitely bad. He looked up towards the heavens for inspiration and instead saw he was no more than ten feet from Brad's Gun Shop.

He'd never owned a gun in his life and he'd never wanted to, but life had changed. He knew he couldn't get a handgun immediately, but he was pretty certain he'd be able to buy a shotgun on the spot. He walked up to the door and peered inside. The store was empty except for a middle-aged man in a camouflage hat behind the counter smoking a cigarette and reading a magazine. Charley could see an array of handguns and rifles neatly displayed in racks behind the counter. Everything he could possibly want to blow away a dwarf and a mobster. Just as he was about to go into the store, a big black SUV pulled into a parking space, fifteen feet from the diner. Charley took one look and began to run.

"Look," said Eduardo, pointing out the window. "That looks like a restaurant of some sort. Not a great one I am sure, but we have to eat, Bobby."

"Yeah, you're right. I'm starving. I don't even remember when we last ate a proper meal."

It was true. In their rather hasty departure from Chicago Joe's, they hadn't even had an opportunity to grab a bread roll, and had sustained themselves on chips and peanuts from the gas station where they'd stopped to fill up.

"This looks like it's going to be as good as we can get around here. But let's be quick. Our only way out of this, Eduardo, is to get to Fanny before Nano and Sammy do."

As they were about to enter the diner, a figure sped by them and disappeared through the door, nearly knocking Eduardo to the sidewalk.

"How uncouth," said Eduardo, dusting himself off. "What kind of clientele frequent this place? I hope they can make a decent pasta."

It took him all of twenty seconds after walking in to realize he was out of luck. The casual observer may have been for two minds as to whether Fanny was more shocked to see Eduardo or vice versa, but shocked they both were. Eduardo gaped at Fanny and Fanny, despite the half-eaten fry that occupied a portion of her mouth, gaped right back at him.

"Don't come any closer," yelled Charley, picking up the rather blunt knife from his placemat. A few diners turned around to observe the scene, but none seemed particularly worried. When strange folk came to Eureka, strange things happened. It was best to just ignore them.

"Relax," said Bobby, who read the situation faster than his father would have given him credit for. "Sit down, we just want to talk."

"Right," replied Charley. "Is that a euphemism for 'kill'?"

"Jesus, who do you think we are?"

"I know who you are, and I know what you're planning to do to us."

"In that case you have me at a disadvantage. I know who she is but I don't know who you are, and whatever it is that you think Eduardo and I were going to do to you is probably wrong. So why don't we sit down and just talk."

While Charley and Bobby were squaring off, Eduardo slid into the booth opposite Fanny. Neither said a word and Fanny stared down at her plate. Suddenly Eduardo reached out for her hand, which he yanked towards his mouth and attempted to kiss.

"Fanny, please, can you forgive me? This is all my fault. I should have paid you even if you wouldn't have beautiful sex with me. And trust me, it would have been beautiful." He grimaced suddenly as his still painful scrotum and adjacent appendages reacted to the thought.

If Fanny hadn't pulled her hand away as quickly as she did, Charley would probably have stabbed Eduardo with the blunt knife. But he paused as Fanny looked up.

"It is all your fault, Mr. Sabatini. You hired me to be a belly dancer, not a whore. And I am not a whore. But you wouldn't listen to me. So I'm sorry I took the book, and as far as I'm concerned you can have it back. But you have to pay me what you owe me for my time."

"Of course, I will pay you, my dear. And, please, call me Eduardo. But I would also ask you, no, entreat you to reconsider my offer back in Rome."

"Absolutely not, Eduardo. There is nothing to reconsider." She leaned into Charley and put her head on his shoulder. "This is the man I am with."

Charley grinned. He couldn't help himself.

Eduardo looked both hurt and offended. "And who might you be, sir?"

"It doesn't matter who I am. All you need to know is that if you harm a hair on Fanny's head I will probably, uh, most likely kill you."

"Unless I probably kill you first, which of course I would have no trouble doing after my extensive experience."

"Okay, stop," said Bobby, who seemed to be the only person with his emotions under control. "Eduardo, I've only known you a few days, but I think it's pretty obvious that you haven't killed anyone other than your governess...." He looked at Charley and Fanny. "It's a long and sordid story that he can tell you when we have more time. But you...," he said this to Charley, "are not going to do much with a blunt knife. So, let's stop all this talk of killing and whoring ... apologies, Fanny. We are all in the same boat at this moment. So let's put our cards on the table."

He was interrupted by the waitress, who shoved two menus in front of him and Eduardo, and stood by while they scanned the menu. Bobby looked at the hamburgers that Fanny and Charley were eating and asked for the same. Eduardo, after rolling his eyes, reluctantly ordered one too, but also asked for an expresso.

"Best I can do, hon, is give you a coffee real fast." And with that she slopped the dark liquid from the black-topped Bunn pot into his mug, spilling a glob on his cream slacks but fortunately missing his scalded appendage.

There was an awkward silence. Then Charley took a sip of his root beer float and looked up at Bobby.

"Okay, I agree. Let's put our cards on the table. You go first."

"Fine, but we're going to have to be quick: there are two of the most dangerous lunatics you can possibly imagine after us. All four of us. And they have nothing pleasant in mind other than killing you, and us. So, here are my thoughts. You clearly seem to know who I am and no doubt Fanny has filled you in on Eduardo?

"Right, so far."

"I'm not sure how you know who I am, but you can tell me later. What's more important is who you are and why you're even involved in this?"

"Fair enough. My name is Charley Brooks. I'm a writer ... and I was a war correspondent, by the way, and could have done serious damage with this knife if I used some of the tricks I learned from a Hazara fighter in Afghanistan...." Charley waved the knife at Eduardo, who didn't seem overly impressed. He was too busy swooning over Fanny. "I met Fanny at that restaurant in LA where your goons were attempting to kidnap her, and I can't believe I'm saying this to you, but I fell in love with her. And I'm not going to leave her."

At the mention of love, Eduardo let out a slight whimper and shook his head. "Ah, Fanny. Please tell me this is not so? That there is still hope for us?"

"It is so, Eduardo," said Fanny firmly. "There is zero hope for us. Or I should say, more accurately, for you."

"Fine, fine," said Bobby. "Though I have to tell all of you I'm not sure how much of what I've heard over the past few days is real or bullshit. So, let's just move on. We're wasting time. We need to get the book and we need to work out a way to get it to Eduardo's uncle, and we need to do it in a place or from a place where they can't just kill us."

"You have our map. So you know where we're heading."

"Yes," said Bobby. "Worland, Wyoming. I imagine that's where this damn book is."

"It's with my mom in Worland," said Fanny. "I sent it to her when I got to Los Angeles. That's where Charley and I are going, and I think it's the safest place. My mom has protection."

"What sort of protection?" asked Bobby.

"I think they're all off-duty cops or prison guards."

"I don't get it, why does your mother need them?"

Before Fanny could answer, Charley jumped in. "Let's just say for some of the same reasons your dad needs protection. The Packer name carries a lot of weight in that area and you don't fuck around with them. As far as I can tell, the Packer Family is one of the most powerful families in the Northwest."

"The only family in the Northwest are the Colacurcios in Seattle. I've never heard of the Packer Family. And I think I'd know."

"Clearly you don't. And the reason you don't is why you should not mess with them. Very secretive and extremely deadly."

Bobby looked at Charley with a quizzical expression. "I don't really believe you, but it doesn't matter. Because I promise you this: off-duty cops and prison guards are not going to stop Nano Mortale or Sammy

'Peppers.' Our only chance is to get there as quickly as possible, grab the book, and then get off the radar before they know where we are. Maybe we keep going north to Canada."

"I'm not sure," said Fanny, who'd realized what Charley was doing. "How do Charley and I know you won't just kill us and then take the book?"

"Fanny, my darling." Eduardo tried once again to take her hand but she pulled away quickly. "You know I could never hurt you. It is not within me."

"Oh, excuse me," Charley interrupted him. "I thought you had tons of experience in the field of killing?"

Bobby slammed his hand down on the table, narrowly missing the hamburgers that the waitress had just placed in front of him and Eduardo. "I said cards on the table and I mean it. Eduardo and I are not killers. That's the reason our families want to take us out. We're an embarrassment to them. Getting the book back and killing you two was our last chance. And both my father and Eduardo's uncle knew that there was no way we'd be able to kill you. They needed us to find you because Nano and Sammy may not even be capable of reading a map between the two of them. So now we're as dead as you are. Or will be unless we can work together. I'm not sure exactly where Nano and Sammy are, but I can't imagine they're far behind us. They would have got as much help as they needed from the Bonannos and some crooked cops in LA."

And so between mouthfuls of hamburger and fries, the hunters who'd now become the hunted, and the hunted who continued to be the hunted, made their plan to work together. It might have been too late if the Cadillac driven by Nano Mortale hadn't been stopped by a Utah state trooper.

Sammy, whose arm was in a sling, was not happy. He'd tried his best to be considerate in the way he delivered the don's resolve to kill Bobby and Eduardo. What thanks had he got? Petulance, betrayal, and a round of buckshot in his shoulder from the real rat at the next table. Still the Bonnanos had been so grateful to discover "No Balls" Boschetto in the same restaurant that they'd taken Sammy to their family doctor and loaned him and Nano a Cadillac Coup De Ville, with a souped-up engine that they assured Sammy had enough power to take on any chase. But on top of everything they had had to deal with the state trooper, who had thought that Nano, because his head was below the steering wheel, was a child wearing a porkpie hat. It was a mistake he'd regret for a long time.

# CHAPTER 22

The road to Worland.

*Why do most accidents happen close to home?*

Twenty minutes after their extremely accommodating waitress had agreed to keep the Mustang safely in her garage for twenty dollars a month, with two months up front, Charley and Fanny found themselves in the backseat of the black SUV on the way to Worland. Fanny had called her mom, who didn't seem too perturbed at the potential apocalypse racing towards her establishment, and had even promised to have extra security close at hand in case it was needed. Charley had reluctantly agreed to call Paula and tell her where they were leaving the car.

"I don't really care that much about the car," Paula had said. "But I do care about Fanny." The transition to Portia was seamless. "I really should have listened to my gut. You are clearly not to be trusted. You're weak and useless...."

"Hang on a second, Portia...."

"What did you call me?"

"Uh, Paula?"

"No, you sniveling little worm. You called me Portia. I knew there was something about you."

"There's nothing about me ... I just slipped up."

"Liar! You've seen my publications or my ads, haven't you?"

"Well, I did see something but only when I was trying to find Fanny?" He regretted that the minute he said it.

"Trying to find Fanny...? I thought you said you saw her for the first time in the restaurant? Hah! I've caught you out, haven't I? Well, I am going to have to tell Fanny that you're a fraud."

"No. Please, Paula, I don't have time to explain. I promise I am not a fraud and I will explain when I see you again back in Los Angeles."

"You're not getting out of this, you dirty little pervert. I'm flying to Worland today. I'll see you there this evening. And I will get the truth out of you. That's my promise."

Charley was still pale looking out the window at the passing highway. If Portia spilled the beans and Fanny realized his "serendipitous" encounter with her had actually been premeditated, it could change everything. And he couldn't allow that to happen. It wasn't right. He didn't know what he'd do if he lost Fanny now.

"What's wrong with you?" asked Bobby from the driver's seat.

"Nothing, really. Just a bit of unsavory news...."

"You mean worse than the fact that two crazy bastards are about to cut off your noggin?"

"How was Paula, Charley?" Fanny asked, ignoring Bobby. "Was she okay about the car?"

"Yes, no problem about the car, but she's coming to meet us in Worland. Fanny, there's something I have to tell you."

Before Fanny could ask what it was, Bobby interrupted. "Who's coming to meet us in Worland?

"My friend Paula," Fanny replied, picking up Paula's map from the console. "The woman you stole this map from."

Eduardo, who'd been in a funk since Fanny had rejected him in the diner, perked up. "The women in the house? The big woman with ice in her veins? I met this woman. She is magnificent, but dangerous."

"You got that right," Charley said, thinking about what was in store for him if they ever reached Worland.

"Well, I am very keen to see her again. Out first meeting was full of misunderstandings."

"And scalded testicles. Jesus, Eduardo! Why would you want to see her again?"

"You wouldn't understand, Bobby my friend." Admittedly it had been painful at the time. Yet the more thought about her, the more he realized just how much he needed her. Had he known he would get to see this Paula again, he never would have made advances on Fanny.

"Don't worry, Eduardo," Fanny chimed in, as if reading his mind. "I'm sure you'll get along again. In fact, I'm thrilled you might fancy someone else, because I have someone and I'm not letting him go. Now, Charlie, what did you want to tell me?"

Charley looked at her and choked. Any courage or guilt or whatever emotion had released the internal truth serum vaporized. He smiled and squeezed her hand. "It wasn't anything important, Fanny."

"Good, because I have something to tell you too, but I'd rather it waited until we get to my mom's place." Fanny looked out the window as if she were deep in thought.

They drove in silence for about ten minutes until Charley couldn't stand it. "What sort of car do they have, Bobby? We need to make sure no one's following us."

"I don't know," Bobby replied, his eyes darting to the rearview mirror. "Probably something fast and flashy. They may even go for a sports car because they don't have luggage. It's all in the back of this thing. In fact, Charley, why don't you take a look inside their bags? You may find some guns, and I'd feel better if we had a few. The big black duffle and the smaller grey one."

"You're telling me that you guys don't have guns?"

"No," said Eduardo. "I am not fond of guns. I have only fired one once when I was about five years old. I found my father's Beretta in the desk drawer and blew the nose off a bust of one of my ancestors. My father was not happy. What about you, Bobby?"

"I hate guns too. I mean I know how to shoot, but I've never seen the need to carry one. They totally mess up the line of your suit, no matter how good your tailor is. Although, I wish I had one now."

"I have to say," spoke up Fanny, "you're not exactly classic mobsters as I understand the word. No wonder everyone is after you."

Bobby snorted. Eduardo looked hurt.

Meanwhile, Charley had leaned over the backseat and opened the large black duffle.

"What the hell is all this stuff?"

"That's Nano's bag. It weighs a ton."

"Well, it's full of tubes or pipes of some sort. I can't see any guns. What does he do? Use different pipes on different occasions to kill people?"

"No, idea. Eduardo? What are those pipes in Nano's bag?"

Eduardo slowly turned around and looked at one of the three-foot-long pipes that Charley was holding up. "I am not familiar with them. He brought them all the way from Rome, so they must have significance. Probably to torture you before he pops your head like an overripe zucchini, which I hate to have to tell you is his specialty."

"Well, there's not much we can do with those," Charley said, zipping up the larger duffle and reaching for Sammy's. He started to go through it and stopped suddenly. "What the hell? Are you sure this is Sammy's?" He held up a pair of pink panties.

Bobby saw what he was holding up in the back mirror and swerved dangerously. "Oh, my God, Sammy wears women's underwear. I thought there was something odd about the dude."

"And he has quite a variety," Charley said, pulling out three more pairs.

Fanny grabbed them and held them up. They were very large and blocked Bobby's view of the road behind. "You know these would fit me perfectly, and they're a lot nicer than the ones I bought at Walmart."

"You can't wear them, Fanny. It's too weird."

"Why would it be weird? They're perfectly clean."

"Well, it's just like if you wear underwear from a man who wears women's underwear then technically you're wearing men's underwear."

"That doesn't make any sense, Charley. You're just being idiotic. But if it makes you uncomfortable, I'll put them away."

"Well, what are we going to do with them?" Charley asked as Fanny put them back in the suitcase.

"I'll tell you exactly what...." Bobby turned around with a huge grin on his face. "This could be the break we need. "If Sammy knows that we know he wears panties, then we have an incredible advantage. That sort of behavior is frowned upon in the mafia. They'll probably break his knees at the very least."

"My uncle," chimed in Eduardo, who seemed to have gotten into the spirit of the discovery, "wouldn't be that nice. He'd cut off Sammy's dick and shove it down his throat."

"Oh, my lord," said Fanny. "Listen to you, people. Do you not have any decency or compassion? So what if he likes to wear woman's underwear? It doesn't make him a bad person?"

"No, but the fact that he kills people while wearing women's underwear kind of does. Look, now you know why Eduardo and I want nothing to do with our families. They're all fucking crazy. Killing people is perfectly acceptable. But crossdressing, or wanting to live your own life, is a capital offence."

"I totally get why you want to do this, but how you think you can pull it off is kind of confusing," Charley said. "If we're going to have any chance of getting out of this alive, then you're going to have to explain how you see things panning out. I mean, how are you going to use the lingerie against Sammy? He'll kill you before the threat of blackmail is out your mouth."

"Sammy's not that bright. He'll take any threat as something very real. I think I can pull it off before he tries to whack me."

"I hope you're right, but it's not much of a plan."

"No, to be honest we haven't had much of a plan for anything. It's all happened too fast. But if you've got any thoughts, I'm totally open."

"We don't," Fanny said. "There are just too many variables at this stage. I would say planning anything longer than five minutes out is impossible. We're committed to driving to Worland with you and returning the book. Hopefully when we get there we'll be safer, and have a little breathing space to decide what to do. But I still know nothing about this mysterious book, and as far as I'm concerned, this whole thing could still be a trap. I am familiar enough with mafia and omertà to know you can't just leave the family...."

"Well," said Eduardo, "first of all, omertà has nothing to do with leaving the family. Omertà is about keeping your mouth shut tight. Secondly, the title of don does not necessarily pass from father to son. In my case, the title went from my father to my uncle when my father and mother were killed by the Camorra from Naples. I believe my uncle was behind it so he could take over. He would love to have me dead, but he believes, or believed, I was the key to the book. Now that the book has gone, he has no reason to want me alive."

"Well, I'm still at the disadvantage here," said Charley. "You all seem to know what makes the book so special. I have no idea what it is."

"I don't either," Fanny chimed in. "As I told you at Paula's house, it looked like an old codex. I didn't understand the language and the illustrations were quite odd. Not something done by some celibate monk in a lonely monastery. All I wanted was something to cover what you owed me, Eduardo."

"So you did look in the book?"

"Just the first few pages."

"What do you mean by 'odd'?" asked Charley

Eduardo turned round and tried, rather unsuccessfully, to take Fanny's hand. "She means the illustrations are of people making love in strange and exotic positions. The book is written in ancient Greek. It has been in my family for over five hundred years. Where it was before, that we don't know. It was, when the lawyer gave it to me, accompanied by instructions which, while easy to understand, also come with a warning about who should use the book and who should not. The reason I am the key is most probably because of my incredible virility. Which I might add is legendary in Rome. The text indicates that the man must be in the prime of his sexual performance, as I could have demonstrated, Fanny, if you'd let me. But it is too late now, I'm afraid. I will have to show your friend Paula."

"Well, I'm happy not to have experienced your incredible virility, as you put it, and you have my permission to be with Paula. Though quite frankly it sounds like a load of garbage." Much to Charley's surprise, Fanny opened the suitcase and began to reexamine the various pieces of lingerie.

"Fanny's right," Charley said, getting more flustered. "That makes absolutely no sense whatsoever,"

"It makes perfect sense. The book is an ancient text about immortality and how to achieve it."

Charley shook his head. "Jesus, you mean we've gone through all of this with the threat of death hanging over our soon-to-be severed heads for a load of rubbish?"

"It is far from rubbish. It is very real. Believe me, I know."

"Really? First of all, there's no such thing as immortality, and secondly, if your family has had it for so long, how come none of your ancestors achieved it? Unless you're going to tell us that you're four-hundred years old, of course."

"He's right, Eduardo," Bobby said. "We're in this situation because of some stupid work of fiction and it's actually quite fucking annoying."

"You are all wrong because you don't understand, not even you, Bobby, how Italian men think. I am telling you Italian men believe that even at seventy they are at the pinnacle of their virility. And so most of my ancestors, the men I mean, kept the book hidden from the younger generation, because they were

certain they could find the right woman and forni-
cate their way to immortality. They were wrong. So
by the time the next generation inherited the book,
they were mostly too old. And if you have tried any of
the positions in the book, you will know what I mean.
If they don't cripple you, they will kill you ... as my governess found out."

"So why did you lie to me about wanting a belly
dancer? What made you think I'd be a good partner
for this, if you don't mind me saying, insane idea?"
Fanny asked.

"The text specifies a particular type of woman. And
you fit the description perfectly."

"I don't believe you, Eduardo."

"You may believe what you like, my dear. But it is
true. I tried with many women in the past but none
who epitomized the curves and the hair and the lips
of the woman described in the text as well as you. But
it is too late now. In any case, I would rather spend
an hour with this Paula than a thousand lifetimes without her."

Silence descended on the SUV as each of the passengers appeared to think about what Eduardo had
said. Eduardo, least of all as he was now fully focused
on meeting Paula, aka Portia, Princess of Pain. For
him, immortality had taken a backseat to immorality.

Whatever was going through their collective minds
distracted them from the imminent danger of a large
black Cadillac speeding up behind them. The driver
was a dwarf in a porkpie hat. It was only when the
Cadillac pulled up alongside and tried to force the

SUV off the road that the full extent of their situation jolted them back to reality.

"Jesus, what the hell is this lunatic trying to do?" said Bobby, who hadn't quite realized who was in the Cadillac.

"It's them," Eduardo screamed. "It's Nano and Sammy."

The Cadillac smashed into the SUV once again, tearing off the front bumper and pushing the big black van onto the gravel. "Shoot them, Charley," Eduardo whimpered as he slid down in the seat.

"With what, you idiot? There wasn't a gun in Sammy's bag. Look, he's the one with the gun." Charley had attempted to push Fanny down—an almost impossible task—and was doing his best to stay low as he tried to make out what was happening in the Cadillac. He could see the awful face of Nano Mortale grinning at him from beneath the porkpie hat as he swung the Cadillac back into the SUV with a bone-jarring crunch. He could also see an enormous man in the passenger seat whom he assumed was Sammy "Peppers." The giant's right arm was in a sling, and he appeared to be having a lot of trouble deciding which hand to use to hold an automatic that looked big enough to stop a rampaging elephant. Sammy finally settled on the sling-arm, and in an extremely unprofessional move for a hitman, fired the gun.

The bullet passed through Nano's hat, narrowly missing the top of his head, shattering his window and deflecting into the passenger mirror on the SUV, sending it sliding into the grass on the side of the road. It was all Bobby could do to keep the SUV moving forward. Charley had ducked down, but Fanny, much to his horror, clambered over him, crushing him into the seat, and began to wave a pair of the panties at Sammy, who was taking aim again, this time with his left hand.

"Hold up the cellphone too," said Bobby, who had remained remarkably calm and was doing his best to keep the SUV on the road. "He'll think you're calling my dad."

It was a good ploy in that Sammy "Peppers'" face contorted into an excellent rendition of Munch's *The Scream*, and he lowered the gun.

"He's putting the gun away," Fanny said, taking another pair of panties and Charley's cellphone and waving them at Sammy, who looked—though it was hard to tell from where she sat on top of a prone and pained Charley—as if he were now about to burst into tears. It was however also a bad ploy in that Bobby relaxed his grip on the steering wheel just as Nano, who didn't seem to have been in the least bit bothered by the gunshot or the appearance of the lingerie, rammed the front of the SUV in precisely the right spot, sending it into a mad swerve that took it from the pavement to the gravel, back onto the grass and seconds later into a large, rather unfortunately situated Cottonwood tree.

Had any occupants not been wearing seatbelts, they would have been beyond any of the fiendish tortures they imagined Nano and Sammy had planned for them. But luckily they were only badly jolted. Bobby tried to restart the SUV, but the hundred-foot tall Cottonwood that had integrated itself into the

SUV's hood had caused major damage to both mechanicals and electricals, and the engine refused to turn over. By this time the Cadillac had pulled up on the shoulder and both predators were advancing on their slightly dazed prey, who had unwittingly, and perhaps stupidly, exited the wreck.

"We're dead," said Bobby. "We're fucking dead."

"Not yet," Charley responded under his breath. "They still need the book."

Further reassurance was abruptly cut off as both Nano and Sammy arrived at the scene with awful grins on their faces. For a minute, no one said anything.

"You shouldn't have done what you did, Bobby. It wasn't very nice. And the Bonannos, by the way, think you're extremely rude for not coming over to say hello." Sammy held the automatic in his left hand.

"I don't know what you wanted me to do, Sammy. Just sit back and let you kill me? Eduardo and I had no choice."

"Of course. I understand. But it would have been nice and easy. Which is how I prefer things in a killing situation. Now look what's happened. Because of you, I'm shot in my arm. So now it's going to be hard, and it's not going to be much fun for me or you. I could shoot you right now, but I can't shoot straight with my left hand. I'm frankly a little confused as to how to kill you. I suppose I'm going to have to use my knife, and that's messy."

"Why don't you just forget about it then? Tell my dad and Eduardo's uncle that you killed us. We'll disappear, I promise."

"I can't do that, Bobby. It wouldn't be honest."

"Honest...? Are you fucking kidding me? You're a hitman, for Christ's sake. And you wear woman's underwear. When did you suddenly develop morals?"

"The underwear is a gift for my girlfriend. They're not mine."

"Bullshit. What? Does your girlfriend weigh three-hundred pounds? Those are yours."

"Shut up, Bobby. They're not mine."

"Oh, right. Then prove it. Pull down your pants and show us your underpants."

"Absolutely not."

"Then I don't believe you. You are a crossdresser. I called my dad to tell him. You're in big shit, Sammy. He wants you back immediately."

"You didn't call him, Bobby. And even if you had, you may as well know the truth: it doesn't worry me. Your dad loves my choice of lingerie. In fact, he buys them for me."

"What the hell are you talking about?"

"What do you think I'm talking about?"

"I have no fucking idea. I suppose you're going to tell me that my dad and you are lovers...."

"Bobby, I tell you this only because I am going to kill you. Yes, your dad and me, we are in love. We have been ever since your mom died."

"You're lying...."

"I'm not. I promise you."

"That's impossible. The two of you ... I'm sorry it makes no sense."

"Why? Just because we are tough men? You think all gay men have to be effeminate like Eduardo over there?"

"How dare you?" Eduardo took an indignant step over to Sammy. "I am an extreme heterosexual. Just because a man is refined and sensitive doesn't make him gay."

That's where Fanny jumped in. "I've never heard such absolute crap in my life. No one cares if you're all gay or not. What the hell has that got to do with anything you're about to do? Sammy, why don't you and Nano just get back in your car and drive away and stop acting like hoodlums."

Charley may have been fascinated by the totally bizarre conversation were he not focused on keeping himself between Fanny and Nano. The dwarf was staring at Fanny as if he were contemplating a giant banana-cream pie. He licked his lips, exposing the most horrific set of teeth Charley had ever seen. His heart sank as he realized there was no possible way he could ever stop the deadly assassin. All he could do was throw himself at Nano and hope his own death would give Fanny the time she needed to escape into the trees.

For the moment, Charley's bravado appeared to be working. Nano paused and turned his full attention to Eduardo. He bounded over, grabbed Eduardo by both ears, and began to twist them wildly.

"No, Nano, no, please," shrieked Eduardo as the dwarf gave a blood-curdling grunt and began to squeeze his head.

That was when Fanny did the bravest thing Charley had ever witnessed.

Or the most stupid.

She pushed Charley aside and rushed up to Nano. "No," she said, smacking the dwarf on the back. "No, bad monkey."

"Ow, ow," wailed Eduardo as his face began to go red.

"Stop, monkey, stop!" ordered Fanny, slapping Nano even harder on the back.

"Don't make him any madder," shouted Charley, trying to pull Fanny away. "Don't call him monkey. For God's sake, Fanny."

"Why?" Fanny gave the dwarf another mighty whack, which did the trick. He let go of Eduardo's head and turned slowly towards Fanny and Charley with a grimace that froze Charley, who was in the midst of flinging himself at Fanny to push her aside. Nano raised his lips, exposing his awful choppers, and then he stopped. His face seemed to soften, and he pushed his lower lip forward as though he was a child being admonished by his mother, or an old man about to eat soup. He opened his arms and, to everyone's total astonishment, embraced Fanny. His grunts turned to soft gurgling coos and his eyes filled with tears.

"Can't you see, he's not a little man? He's a big monkey."

Nano put his head on Fanny's shoulder and attempted to kiss her on the lips. "No, monkey, no kissee on the lips, just the cheek. See...."

She turned to Charley and Eduardo, whose eyes were moving up and down in an alarming fashion. His head had started bleeding again from the wound he'd sustained two nights before and he was muttering incoherently.

"See, he's perfectly calm now. I bet he's been abused and that's what makes him go crazy enough to want to kill. Don't worry, monkey, you're safe now." She squeezed Nano's shoulders.

"He's not a monkey," said Sammy, who appeared to have given up trying to figure out how to kill Bobby.

"What?"

"He's an orangutan."

"What the hell are you talking about Sammy? He's a hitman, Nano Mortale, the Deadly Dwarf." Eduardo had recovered enough to understand what was being said. "He is my uncle's most trusted killer."

"He is. He has never failed your uncle, or Bobby's father for that matter. Saved both their lives on many occasions. They rescued him from a terrible situation in a roadside circus in Italy. You know how your father loves animals, Bobby. He couldn't stand to see a creature being tortured. So he and Don Sabatini killed the circus owner and took Nano away with them. He was trained to be a killer by the famous female assassin, Conchita Palomino, who from what I've been told, must have looked a lot like Fanny."

Nano had removed his hat and coat and was trying to hump Fanny, who was doing her best to fend off his advances. "No, monkey. You can't have sex with me. Put that thing back in your pants." Charley saw that Nano's two-inch penis was sticking out of his fly.

"Jesus, that's a tiny penis," said Bobby.

"Don't say that," yelled Sammy as Nano turned his attention from Fanny to Bobby. The orangutan leapt at Bobby and flung him to the ground. "He's very sensitive about the size of his dick."

"Stop, monkey, stop." There was a firmness to Fanny's voice, almost as if she was channeling Portia. "Bobby didn't mean there's anything wrong with your penis. It's a beautiful little penis, and I am sure any female monkey would love it."

"Yes," wailed Bobby as Nano slammed his face into the ground. "It's beautiful. Stop, please." Nano took a step back and held his little appendage up to Bobby, who was now sitting up. Nano began to grunt in an alarming way.

Once again it was Fanny who came to the rescue. "No, monkey. Leave Bobby. We'll find you a nice lady monkey in Worland. I promise."

Whether or not Nano understood what Fanny was saying was unclear, but he tucked his penis back in his pants and went to stand next to her.

"Look," said Charley, deciding someone had to take charge. "No one needs to have sex with or kill anyone. This whole situation is ludicrous. Fanny and I just want to be together. Bobby, you and Eduardo want to get as far away from your respective relatives as possible. Nano needs to find an orangutan mate, and Sammy, I'm not sure what you want. I suggest we go to Worland, get the book, and then Sammy, if you want, you can take it back to Don Casagrande and tell him you killed us. How does that sound?"

The others nodded, but Sammy looked worried. "It's not going to work. I have to bring him some heads."

"That is so old school, Sammy," Bobby said, raising his hands in frustration. "What's with this violence you seem so focused on? Just take the book and tell him you blew us up with a car bomb."

"That's good, Bobby. That may work. But I still have to have some proof. Maybe I can just take one head." He pulled a large switchblade from an ankle-sheath with his left hand and advanced on the group. He looked at Bobby, Eduardo, and Charley in turn and then focused on Fanny. "I'm sorry, miss, but I think your head is the one they wanted originally. So it's gotta be you."

"You don't have to do this, Sammy." Charley jumped in front of Sammy and tried to push him away.

But Sammy, despite his incapacity, was on a mission. He flung Charley aside and made a grab for Fanny. She screamed as he pulled her down onto the ground and put his huge leg on her back to hold her still while he put the switchblade to her throat

If Sammy could have taken more time to reflect on it, he might have come to the conclusion that it wasn't a very bright move. There was a bloodcurdling screech, and Nano leapt onto Sammy's back, knocking him off Fanny and onto his stomach. He took Sammy's head in his powerful hands and began to squeeze. Eduardo, Bobby, and Charley watched in abject horror, and Fanny, who'd recovered from the sudden onslaught, yelled for Nano to stop. But Nano was beyond mere commands. Sammy was gurgling and his face, which had been a dark shade of red to begin with, turned purple.

"Stop, Nano. Please don't kill him." Fanny managed to take hold of Nano's right paw and was trying her best to tug it off Sammy's rapidly flattening skull. "You have to stop, Nano. You have to stop with all the killing." She began to sob. Tears began to roll down her cheek as the sobs turned to moans. She rolled onto her back and her body began to convulse as if she were in deep pain.

Nano stopped what he was doing. He stood up and walked over to where Eduardo and Bobby were watching the bizarre scene and slung a hairy arm around Bobby's shoulder. No one said a word as Charley knelt next to Fanny and cradled her head.

"It's okay, Fanny. It's okay, my love. He's stopped."

"It's all my fault, Charley. Everything is my fault. If I hadn't been so stupid, none of this would be happening." She put her arms round Charley and dragged him down till his head came into contact with a heaving breast.

"No, it's not. It's not your fault." Charley felt the familiar electricity rip through his body as if he'd touched a live wire. "Oh, Fanny. This is nearly over. No one's going to kill anyone now, I promise. And if you hadn't have done what you did, how would we have met? Fanny, you are the smartest, bravest, most beautiful person I've ever known."

He tried to lift himself off her, but she clung onto him as if she'd found the very thing she'd been searching for. And at that moment any doubt or hesitation about what it was she felt for Charley vanished.

Eduardo wandered over to Sammy, who was still lying on the ground babbling like an idiot. He tried to pull Sammy up and Bobby came over to help. They got him into a semi-standing position, but it was obvious that something was dramatically wrong with Sammy "Peppers." His head was now curiously misshapen, like that of Pip or Flip, the Pinheads who once headlined at the Coney Island Freak Show.

"Dear God, is he okay?"

Sammy managed to pull himself upright, but his eyes were glazed and a steady groan emanated from somewhere deep in his enormous body. He began to wander off till he hit a tree and fell over again. Bobby rushed over, helped him up, and then steered him towards the Cadillac, where he put him on the backseat. Sammy promptly fell asleep.

"What should we do now?" asked Eduardo. "The one car seems damaged beyond repair, and the Cadillac cannot accommodate all of us."

In the end, they called Fanny's mom, who agreed to send the Bookmobile from Worland, which as it turned out was only two hours away from the crash scene.

# CHAPTER 23

Packer's Hard-Back Books and Soft-Back Women. The World's only Brothel and Lending Library.

*When you drink from Fountain of Youth, take small sips.*

It was nearly seven o'clock in the evening when the Bookmobile pulled into the parking lot of the Packer Brothel and Lending Library. The truck had no passenger seats, so Charley had been forced to spend the entire journey leaning against one of the bookshelves and his back was killing him. Eduardo and Bobby, who were in a different section, looked equally miserable, but Nano, who'd gone back to full-on ape, was having a merry time taking books off the shelves and flinging them through the sliding windows at passing cars. There was one rather gaudy bedroom towards the back of the vehicle, which Fanny explained was still used every now and then when the Bookmobile turned back into a travelling brothel. They'd all agreed to let Sammy use the bed, as he'd had a lot of trouble standing since Nano had reshaped his head to resemble an artillery shell. Fanny had insisted on staying with him to make sure he didn't choke on his tongue, which Sammy seemed keen to swallow.

There was a reception committee waiting for them in front of the brothel and Charley recognized Fanny's mom, a tall, statuesque blond with a Dolly Parton hairdo and lips that had suffered at the hands of an overly enthusiastic plastic surgeon. The employees were dressed in their working outfits, which ranged from the usual fishnet stocking and garter-belt ensembles to nurses and policewoman uniforms. A few rough-looking guards armed with shotguns made up the rest of the welcoming party. Much to Charley's relief, Portia was missing. Fanny stepped off the bus first and her mom and the whores rushed up to embrace her. Charley, Eduardo, and Bobby were about to pile out when Nano pushed them aside and leapt from the door to join Fanny. The guards, totally surprised by the orangutan who had taken off everything but his porkpie hat, raised their guns in panic, and would no doubt have fired if Fanny hadn't let out yet another shrill "No!" and rushed up to embrace Nano.

"Don't shoot. He's harmless. Look, he just wants to be loved." The orangutan put his head on her shoulder and grinned at Fanny's mom, who looked quite horrified.

"Fanny, are you sure this is the man you love? He seems a little strange I dare say, and a trite hairy for my taste."

"Oh, Momma, don't be ridiculous. He's an orangutan. This is the man I love. This is Charley. Charley, this is my momma, Miss Flo Packer."

Charley, unsure of exactly how to greet the madam of an impressive brothel, whom he noticed was chewing on either a large piece of gum or a wad of tobacco, took her proffered hand and shook it. "I'm very pleased to meet you, ma'am."

"You don't need to be formal with me, my dear. Just call me 'Miss Flo' like everyone else. Well, Fanny, he's a damn side more attractive than the other guy." She pointed her thumb at Nano, who'd left Fanny's side and gone over to join the demimondes who were quite taken by him. Then her attention was drawn to Eduardo and Bobby, who were standing politely in the background. "And who are these two fine-looking men?"

"I," said Eduardo, stepping up to Flo and taking her hand, "am Eduardo Sabatini, true Marchese di Custoza. I am from Rome, and might I say senora madame di questo bordello, you are perhaps even more stunning than your beautiful daughter." He brought her hand up to his lips and imparted a soft kiss.

"Well, I never," said Flo, who turned as pink as a grapefruit. "Are you sure this isn't a better man for you, Fanny? He has excellent manners obviously, and a sexy accent."

"No, Momma. He's the one who wouldn't pay me in Rome. The one whose book I took."

"You fucking skinflint bastard." Flo spat tobacco juice at Eduardo's feet. "You're no gentleman. How dare you do that to a lady?"

"It was all a terrible misunderstanding, I assure you, Senora. In a thousand years, I would never do anything to harm such a perfect specimen of womanhood as your daughter." Eduardo touched Fanny's cheek with the back of his hand, but leapt back when Nano shrieked at him.

"And I'm Bobby Casagrande, Miss Flo. My father is head of the Casagrade Family in Los Angeles. I believe you're somewhat in the same business, so no doubt you've heard of us?"

Flo looked Bobby up and down. He was certainly a handsome young man, though his hair was disheveled and his white suit wrinkled and stained with blood. He also smelled like he hadn't bathed in a few days. "So your father runs a whorehouse and library in Los Angeles, does he?"

"Um, no ... not exactly. Our family business is more about extortion these days than anything else. Though I believe my grandfather owned a number of discount brothels just outside of Vegas. 'Lay and Pay'? Maybe you heard of them?"

"Nope, never have." Flo had no interest in how other houses operated. Hers ran perfectly fine, thank you very much. She'd once been asked to join the Loyal Order of Madams, which boasted some of the top brothel owner in the country, and which was considered a huge honor, but she'd rather impolitely told them to get lost.

"What I'd love to talk to you about when you get a moment, Miss Flo, is whether you have any openings in your organization. I think I'm going to need a job because I'm not going back to my father. He'll kill me for sure."

"Hmm, well," said Flo, ignoring Bobby's request and taking her daughter by the hand. "There's a lot to think about and discuss. But you're a handsome young buck, so maybe there is something for you. I'll have to test you out."

Bobby blanched.

Miss Flo just laughed. "Don't worry, I'll make sure you pass. All right, it's a quiet night tonight, so we'll all eat dinner together and talk about next steps. By the way, Fanny, your friend Paula flew in a little while ago. She's taking a bath."

"Oh, Jesus," said Charley.

"Thank you, Jesus," said Eduardo.

Packer's Hard-Back Books and Soft-Back Women was an impressive-looking establishment. It resembled an extra-large log cabin and had a similar feel to the Old Faithful Lodge Charley remembered from his childhood when his parents took him to Yellowstone National Park. Charley and party trooped through the front door into a huge reception room that looked out across the Big Horn National Forest and the mountains beyond, which were just beginning to turn purple in the last light of evening.

"Isn't it beautiful, Charley?" Fanny had left her mom's side and come over to Charley, who was staring out the windows, totally mesmerized by the view. She took his arm and snuggled into him, and once again the now familiar current raced through his body making him distinctly lightheaded.

"It is, Fanny. It's quite stunning. I can't believe we're standing here in such an incredible place with no one chasing us or threatening death and dismemberment. I honestly didn't think we'd make it." He put his arm around her shoulder and pulled her closer until the electricity became quite painful.

"I always knew we would. I knew you'd get us here, my darling. And we're safe in this house, I promise. So, why don't we head for my room and we can wash up and change and go down to dinner. And then, if you're not too tired...." Fanny didn't finish the sentence. She didn't need to.

From what Charley could see perusing the books in the library, they did indeed follow the Dewey Decimal classification system. One wall had a segment labelled Vintage Eroticism that included what looked like first editions of *Fanny Hill*, *My Life and Loves*, *A Man with a Maid*, and at least twenty titles that Charley had never heard of. There were two sets of shelves devoted to domination and other fetishes that Charley carefully avoided, and an entire bookcase that had well-thumbed copies of modern erotica. *Filling her Cavity*, *Confessions of a New York Dentist* stood side by side with *Two Genitalmen of Verona, the real Shakespeare*. Charley had pulled out one that involved a lusty plumber unblocking a Los Angeles housewife's drain, and was just enjoying the first paragraph when Flo interrupted him.

"So you found the library, did you?"

Charley spun round to find the madam dressed in a deep purple formfitting dress adorned with ostrich feathers.

"Yes. I didn't want to hang around while Fanny was dressing. I hope you don't mind me coming in here?"

"Nope, you're free to wander where you like, except into the girls' bedrooms. Then I'd probably have to charge you a service fee and kill you for being unfaithful to my daughter. But I don't reckon you'd do that, would you, Charley?" She paused and then answered her own question. "No, I don't think you'd do that. I could see the way you and Fanny looked at each other. You're never going to be able to look at another woman again, are you?"

"I don't think I ever will, Miss Flo. In fact, I know I won't. I wish I could explain it, especially to you. But I can't. I realize Fanny and I have only known each other for a few days, but as you can imagine, they've been a rather eventful few days. Whatever I felt for Fanny before became more intense. It's love for sure. But it also transcends love."

"You can forgo the sentimental explanations, mister. I don't know them and I don't feel them. Never have. Never will. To me men are just a way to make a living. But I know Fanny's different. So don't worry about it. I've known she was different from the day she was born. Not everyone sees it or feels it, though. My mamma believed she was touched by the devil himself, and a lot of the kids at school used to make fun of her. But I've always thought she was special, though I know every mom probably thinks that about their daughters."

"I'm sure you're right, but she is special. I've never met anyone like her before, and I know I never will again. Whatever it is she has is almost mystical or magical. I'm sounding inarticulate once again."

"You are, and I'd say you sound like a damn fool, but I like you, Charley. So why don't you just shut up and enjoy the moment."

Flo walked over to the drinks cart and poured them each a hefty shot of Old Crow bourbon from a large juglike bottle. Charley took a sip and nearly threw up.

"Yeah, it's not the smoothest whiskey, but it's cheap and I like it. Now, Fanny's no doubt told you about her dad, and how she's been searching for him?"

"Well, yes, but I think she realizes she probably won't ever find him."

"No, she won't. I'd like to tell you more about him, but I can't. I don't know squat about him at all, apart from the few things he said and the way he looked. No idea who he was or where he came from. He was a magnificent specimen of a man, I'll tell you that much. Big, handsome alpha male with red lion-mane hair. But big not like the boys who work on the rigs. Rather like some of those ancient statues you see in museums. There wasn't an ounce of fat on his body either, and he made love, Charley ... well let's just say like he was the sun and I was the moon. When he came up, I went down. Fanny may have got her charm from me, but I swear she got whatever else she has from him."

"Well, whatever it is, Miss Flo, I am so madly in love with her."

"You've already said that, Charley. And as I recall I told you to shut up. Now, listen: when Fanny first told me about you and your infatuation—which is what it is because I've seen it before—I was worried. I think she's a beautiful woman, but most of the boys she grew up with thought she was too big. And the ones that didn't, the chubby chasers, held no interest for Fanny. I used to tell her she would know the right guy when he came along. But he never did. So she's never ever had a serious boyfriend. And then suddenly you come along and you fall for her. Just like that." She snapped her fingers to emphasize the point. "Well, that raises a red flag in my book. And it did too for Paula, or Portia as you called her. She told me everything by the way...."

Charley gulped in panic.

"But you don't need to worry about it. You got Fanny here in one piece and that's what counts. So take that threat off the table. And by the way," Flo poured herself another hefty shot of Old Crow, "I think Fanny does put out some 'magical or mystical' vibe, as you put it. There'd have to be something about you to pick it up and not just see her as a big ol' belly dancer. So if she loves you and you love her, then I am good with you too. God knows what the two of you are going to do from here on. I assume you have to stay low for a while?"

"First of all, thanks for seeing it that way because that's exactly the way it is." He thought of *Porky Asses* again and decided it was the one thing about the whole adventure that he probably would never have to worry about again. Unless of course Fanny brought it up. He still believed it was what she wanted to tell him. "As to laying low, yeah, we probably do need to do that until we know whether Eduardo or Bobby's families will come after us. But both families have lost their top hitmen, so maybe they'll just forget the whole thing. I can send the book off to Bobby's dad, anonymously, and hopefully he'll think we're dead and not worth more effort. In terms of what's next, Fanny and I haven't even talked about it. I have money, quite a bit that I inherited from my folks, so money's not an issue. But in truth, I don't know what's next after we send back the book. Where is it, by the way?"

Flo walked over to a shelf on the far wall. "I don't know if you noticed that all these books are of an erotic nature...."

"Yes, it was hard to miss."

"It's in this shelf, the 'How To' section." Flo reached up and pulled out a small leather-bound book sandwiched between *Kama Sutra for Dummies* and *How Not to Suck at Blowjobs, a Beginner's Manual*. "Be real careful, it's quite delicate."

Charley took the book and, as gently as he could, opened it. "Jesus, this must be really old–the pages are vellum."

"Well, I went through it with some of the girls because, if you look carefully, it appears to be some sort of instruction manual on sexual positions. But we tried out a few and they're impossible. Two of the girls suffered terrible vaginal trauma and had to be heavily sedated. Also, I don't know what language it's written in. None of us could make that out."

"Well, surprisingly enough, I do. I know exactly what language this is written in. It's ancient Greek. The language of Aristotle and Sophocles. I studied it for a few semesters."

"Bully for you. Then you can tell us exactly how to do some of those positions without putting our privates into danger."

"I could ... but there's something quite interesting in how it's written. I don't think it's a sex manual. More like an instruction manual on how to get to a higher plane of existence. Which I guess makes sense considering when this was written." Charley began to turn the pages, but Miss Flo smacked his hand.

"You can study it later. Let's go through to the dining room."

Charley stuffed the small book into his pocket as Miss Flo took his arm and led him into a baroquely ornamented dining room that may have seemed out of place in anything other than some antebellum mansion. In a country brothel, however, anything bordering on normal would no doubt have appeared anomalous. An elaborately attired flunky stood with a tray of champagne-filled glasses, which Miss Flo declined and Charley gratefully accepted.

"Oh, Paula, my dear. Can't you at least wait till after dinner to do that?"

Paula, who was in deep conversation with Bobby, was perched on the back of Eduardo, who was on all fours with his face buried in a champagne-filled dog bowl. She looked up at Miss Flo and Charley. "I'm sorry, Miss Flo. I'm trying to teach this worm the consequences of running out on me during a session. But you're right, we can wait till later. Now get up you miserable little bitch, and know that you'll be punished extra hard for this interruption to your training." She gave Eduardo a hard kick with the stiletto heel that completed her full-leather ensemble. Charley shuddered, but Eduardo stood up with a huge grin on his face and greeted Charley as if the situation were entirely normal, which, considering the location and context, probably was.

"Where are Nano and Sammy?" asked Charley, who realized that both the hitman and hit-monkey were missing.

"Sammy is still out for the count, but he's stopped trying to swallow his tongue," replied Bobby, "and Nano is busy assembling those poles that were in his luggage. Apparently, they're part of an elaborate Jungle Gym. I don't know, he seems happy enough, and the ladies are...."

The rest of his sentence hung in the air as all eyes turned to the doorway. Everyone saw Fanny, but Charley saw someone else. If anyone had asked him he would have said Fanny looked beautiful. Yet to say she looked beautiful, he realized, was to say Mount Everest looked tall. Her red hair, incandescent in the soft light cast from the corner sconces, cascaded down on either side of her face, which while devoid of makeup, was devoid of nothing. She wore a green velvet dress that embraced her as if she'd been dipped in mint ice cream, and as Charley stared at her he felt, once again, as if he were in the presence of some empyrean being. She walked up to Charley and touched his face. The familiar sensation that had once felt like a jolt from a cattle-prod now transformed into something entirely different. It filled Charley with energy and sucked the breath from his lungs. He was overcome with an emotion he'd never before experienced, and he felt himself wanting to lie down and leap up at the same time.

"Come, my love," said Fanny. "Sit here, next to me."

Charley said nothing, because there was nothing he could say at that moment. It was as if he were in the room but wasn't. He looked around to see whether any of the others had reacted the same way. If they had, they'd moved on and were eating and drinking and laughing the way one would imagine people who've narrowly escaped death would. Bobby was discussing possible job openings in the Packer organization with Miss Flo, and Fanny and Paula were in deep conversation about the benefits of leather over latex. Eduardo just sat there staring at Portia like a besotted imbecile.

At some point in the meal, of which Charley remembered very little, he sensed someone staring at him. He looked up from his plate into the eyes of Miss Flo, who was sitting at the head of the table. She smiled at him as if she knew precisely what was going on inside his head. He tried to smile back, but his face felt as numb as the rest of his body. Then Fanny squeezed his thigh and the thwack of energy released by her touch pulled him back from whatever plane he'd been on.

"I believe," said Miss Flo, looking directly at Charley, "that it's time for bed. I'm sure most of you are exhausted ... or perhaps stimulated." Here she turned her attention to Eduardo, who had his tongue out like a dog in heat. "So why don't we call it a night and meet for breakfast. Bobby, I'm going to go over the books and also a few new techniques that I'd like the girls to adopt. Perhaps you'd care to join me. I have a feeling this will be a good test of your abilities as our new full-time and only male employee. We can come up with a suitable title while we're at it."

By the time Fanny and Charley got to their room, all semblance of decorum and romantic titillation had been abandoned. Fanny unzipped her dress and stepped out of it. She wore nothing underneath and fell on Charley as he struggled to remove his pants.

"Do you think I have a big ass, Charley?"

"Um, not at all. It seems perfect...."

"You don't think it's porky?

Charley gaped like a largemouth bass. He tried to say something, but no words emerged from his mouth. It didn't seem to matter. Fanny just laughed and pressed her lips to his. Any remnants of the divine vanished as she ground her hips into his crotch. It was as if she could not get close enough to him. They kissed, not lightly, but with an urgency that oozed both lust and hunger. Charley relinquished his struggle to remove his pants and reached around to grasp the object of his initial infatuation. Her bottom was soft and smooth and free of indentation and dimples. He felt lightheaded as the blood rushed from his head to his penis which raged in his pants like a trapped beast. Fanny shifted her weight, unbuckling his belt and pulling his pants down. At that moment the room vanished, and Charley felt himself floating towards a bright light as if he had died.

The saloon of the Occidental Hotel in Buffalo, Wyoming, present day

"What do you mean 'as if you died'?"

"Just that, Barney. I literally died. It was exactly as you'd imagine. I felt myself floating towards this bright light and it was the happiest most glorious feeling you can imagine. It was as if I was swimming in primordial glühwein. Warm and sweet and totally intoxicating, if you can wrap your mind around the metaphor."

"And then?" I wasn't sure how to take what Charley had just told me, let alone what to make of it.

"Well then it was over, and I was back on the bed lying next to Fanny, who appeared to have fallen into a deep sleep. The strangest part was the book that I told you was in my pocket? Well, it had fallen out of my pants when Fanny ripped them off and was next to me digging into my thigh. It was open, as if someone had opened it deliberately. I picked it up and stared at the page. And here's the darndest thing, Barney. The page showed an illustration, surprisingly detailed, like it was done by some monk who painted illuminated manuscripts and moonlighted as an eroticist. You know what I mean...."

"Yes, yes!" I knew I sounded impatient, but my back was killing me from all the sitting and I wanted to get to the end of the story, because while I didn't believe a word of it, I needed a conclusion. Charley carried on as if he hadn't noticed.

"Look, I know you probably think this story defies belief and what I am about to tell you isn't going to make that any better. The illustration, Barney, which was no bigger than a matchbook, was of Fanny."

"You mean someone who looked like Fanny?"

"No, I mean it was Fanny. There was no mistaking her hair, her eyes, and her lips, and of course the other distinctive parts of her fuselage. Which were extremely prominent in the drawing, and therefore quite identifiable. And next to her, or rather entwined in her arms and thighs, in the most remarkable lovemaking position imaginable—or not, for that matter, because I think it would be impossible for ordinary people to imagine at all—was someone who looked like a younger version of me."

"Charley, I hope you don't mind me saying this, but it's sounding a little far-fetched."

"No need to apologize, old man. I get it, believe me. It took me a while to fully understand what was going on. Anyway, there isn't much more to tell. All I'll say is that I began to frantically turn the pages in the book and every illustration, while different in both the elaborateness and degree of difficulty of the positions, was of the same two people. Fanny and me. As if the book were written especially for us. Like we'd lived in another age altogether."

"Are you sure it wasn't just an optical illusion caused by your overly stressed mind? I mean you'd been through a hell of a few days."

"No, it might have been easier if that was the case. It was us. It was incredible, and it's been that way ever since."

I looked closely at my friend and suddenly I knew then what it was I'd seen in the mirror. There was me, a well-lined, jowly, balding overweight sixty-year-old. And then there was Charley, as I remembered him from when we were young men.

"Charley," I said with what must have been a slightly incredulous expression on my face, "whatever it is you're doing here agrees with you. You don't look a day older than when I last saw you. And if anything, you look younger."

He laughed. "That's what I've been trying to tell you. I am younger.... Anyway, I have to go now, Barney. Fanny will be missing me."

"Where? Do you live around here?"

"Well, close, I suppose. It's here, but it's not really. It would be impossible to explain. But I do come down here every few days just to catch up on what's going on in the world."

I desperately wanted to know what he meant, but could see he wasn't going to tell me a whole lot more. It was as if he'd said everything he could. I made one final attempt to get him to stay.

"Come on, Charley, can't you stay a bit longer? I've really missed you. And I want to hear what you're doing now. I'd love to meet Fanny."

"I've missed you too, my friend. But I can't stay. It doesn't work like that. I have to get back or things begin to fall apart. Reverse themselves, if you like. I wish you could meet Fanny. You'd love her, Barney. But you can't. Now I really do have to go. So long."

And with that he smiled, shook my hand, and walked out of the room. But I knew that I couldn't let him go like that. The sudden realization that he looked younger had filled me with a million questions. So I stood up and ambled as fast as I could after him. I saw him for as he walked out the front door of the hotel. He was heading towards a clump of trees. I shouted after him and for a second he turned back and looked at me. He smiled and waved and then he was gone. As if he'd simply vanished into thin air.

I walked back into the bar and ordered a large Maker's Mark from the bartender.

"The guy I was talking to...."

"Yeah?"

"Have you seen him before?"

"Yes, he comes in here maybe once a week, and has a coffee and reads the paper. Been doing it ever since I've been here. That's about ten years. You obviously know him?"

"Well, I did. I haven't seen him for about twenty years, though. He told me a really strange story that I have a hard time believing."

The bartender grinned and rolled his eyes. "I've never really spoken to him other than to take his order, but I promise you I've heard all the stories in these parts. And believe me they're all pretty strange."

"Then maybe you can help me. Ever heard of an establishment called Packer's Soft-Back Women and Hard-Back Books? Supposed to be near Worland...."

"Sure, sure. It was a legendary place."

"Was?"

"Well, it burned down about twenty years ago."

"Jesus, what happened?"

"Supposedly some mob guys from Los Angeles torched it with everyone in it. Real tragedy. Only thing that got out was an orangutan, as I heard. Can't imagine what an orangutan was doing in a whorehouse."

"So everyone else was killed?"

"That's what I heard. Everyone except the orangutan, as I said. He was taken to a local zoo, but they had to put him down when he popped the keeper's head like a giant pimple. You look like you've seen a ghost, my friend. Here...." He poured me another Maker's Mark. "This one's on the house."

The End

69